Y0-CVM-057

THE CAMERA-SHY CUPID

THE CAMERA-SHY CUPID

•

Mary Fanjoy Reid

AVALON BOOKS
THOMAS BOUREGY AND COMPANY, INC.
401 LAFAYETTE STREET
NEW YORK, NEW YORK 10003

© Copyright 1998 by Mary Fanjoy Reid
Library of Congress Catalog Card Number 97-97214
ISBN 0-8034-9284-7
All rights reserved.
All the characters in this book are fictitious,
and any resemblance to actual persons,
living or dead, is purely coincidental.

PRINTED IN THE UNITED STATES OF AMERICA
ON ACID-FREE PAPER
BY HADDON CRAFTSMEN, BLOOMSBURG, PENNSYLVANIA

To my Aunt Audrey, who was the most fascinating redhead I've ever known.

Chapter One

Bree Gaston sat propped up on her elbows reading a television script from the slush pile for the murder mystery series "Sting Like a Bee." She paused to flip back to the bio stapled to the front, and read the name again: Rudolph Gotham. It had to be a pen name, she guessed. But pen name or not, the script definitely had potential. In fact, it was darn good—too good, she thought, to have been written by an amateur.

Bree was writing out her recommendation to the story editing department when George Kane and his manager burst into the room. They came barreling down the narrow aisle, oblivious of the irritated looks the script readers shot out at them from behind the cubicles as they passed. The director of the sitcom "The Camera-Shy Cupid" was complaining loudly.

"I can't work under these conditions!" George Kane threw up his hands dramatically. "Amateurs! All of them! When I say 'close-up,' I don't mean I want to see nose hairs, for Pete's sake! 'Pull back,' I say. They swing so far back the shot looks like we're in another dimension. What do they think we're filming—a *National Geographic* special? You see what I'm saying? You see what I have to deal with?"

His manager tried to calm him with low, gentle words, as a mother might console a misbehaving child. But George Kane was on a roll, and when he was in a mood, as he was today, there was nothing anyone could do about it but let it soar.

"And now you tell me one of my ungrateful extras has defected over to the big leagues! Bah! Everyone wants to be a star these days. Motion pictures, they come and go—but television, television is what keeps America alive! Believe it! Doesn't anyone honor contracts anymore? Gail is all over me about this shooting schedule. So we're two weeks behind? Big deal." He turned to his manager. "Where am I going to find another extra on such short notice?" George Kane hesitated before Bree's cubicle, kneading his brow. "I need to sit down."

Bree heard this roar of a soliloquy, as did everyone else in the reading department, and she turned around, abruptly rising from her chair. "Please, take my seat, Mr. Kane," she said politely, although truthfully she was mildly annoyed by the interruption.

George Kane fell into the chair with a moan. He glanced up at Bree. "You know, when I was younger, I wanted to be a fisherman." His eyes took on a glazed, faraway look. "Out in the fresh air, battling ten-foot waves, catching hooks in the fleshy parts of my arms and legs, laughing with my foul-smelling mates, sitting below-decks playing gin rummy and drinking cheap brandy, cracking crude jokes. You know, all that manly Hemingway stuff. Getting up at the crack of dawn and springing

The Camera-Shy Cupid

out of bed, knowing that the adventures of the day were just about to begin.''

He sighed. ''But look at me.'' He made an exaggerated sweep of his arms. ''Here I am, a director of a *sitcom*.'' He uttered the word ''sitcom'' as if it were a dirty word.

I thought television was what was keeping America alive, thought Bree with a wan smile.

The manager flashed Bree an apologetic smile, and rested his hands on George Kane's slumped shoulders. ''George, we have to be on location in twenty minutes. Casting will take care of the problem. . . .''

George Kane was staring at Bree. He shifted his gaze to the script on her desk. ''Rudolph Gotham,'' he read, shrugging. ''Never heard of him. Good script?''

Bree nodded, and without thinking, she replied, ''It's almost too good for television.''

The director raised his silver-tipped brows. His tiny, keen eyes, shining like two black buttons, scrutinized her with that curious, studious look an entomologist might give to a rare insect. Bree shifted uncomfortably.

''Turn around,'' he said suddenly.

''George—'' began the manager.

Bree frowned, not certain whether to comply or not, to be pleased by this sudden attention—or insulted. She opened her mouth to speak, but George Kane stood up abruptly, stroking his silvery white goatee with his finger thoughtfully. ''Give me a side profile.''

''Uh, Mr. Kane. I—''

But the director was already circling her, pantomiming with his hands the lens of a camera. ''Hmmm . . .'' he said, furrowing his brow. ''I think you'll do.''

''Do? Do for what?'' asked Bree, puzzled.

George Kane nodded and turned to his manager. ''Yes. She'll do fine. Call Casting and tell them I've done their job for them.''

"B-ut . . ." the manager stammered in protest.

"You might as well ride with us, young lady," said George Kane. He glanced at his manager. "She's perfect, don't you think?" And adding before his companion could respond, "It's the red hair. Cheekbones aren't bad. Nice eyes. Put her in something decent and she'll sparkle in front of the camera." This said, George Kane sauntered off down the aisle of cubicles, humming cheerfully to himself.

The manager slipped his hand under Bree's elbow, steering her away from the desk. "We're short an extra actor for the restaurant set of 'The Camera-Shy Cupid,' " he explained quickly. "Have you ever acted on television before?"

"No." Bree shook her head. "I can't just—"

"Don't worry. I'll let the Script Department know you've been hired on as an extra," said the manager.

"Wait . . ." Bree reached under the desk and snatched up her book bag. At the last minute she shoved inside the television script she'd been reading. She wanted to make certain the script arrived safely at Zachary's office with her recommendation; the author deserved as much, she thought, with a determined nod of her head.

"What's your name?" the manager asked her, pulling her briskly along with him.

"Bree Gaston."

The manager mulled this over for a moment, then nodded. "Interesting. A little exotic, maybe—good stage name," he said, directing her into the adjoining corridor. "By the way, my name is Tom Bronfmann. I'm Mr. Kane's manager, baby-sitter, psychiatrist—what have you." Bree laughed, and Bronfmann sighed, gesturing to the older man who was already a good distance ahead of them. The director was moving at a rapid pace, his hands swinging soldierlike at his sides. "If we don't hurry he'll leave without us."

They're all crazy, thought Bree. Couldn't they see that she wasn't an actor? But now as they sprinted down the hall to catch up to the eccentric director, a sudden wave of excitement was sweeping through her. She was going to be on television!

But inside the limousine, the director sat in silence, barely acknowledging her presence. He gazed out the window, distracted by thoughts of his own. Bronfmann, on the other hand, had already produced a laptop computer from his briefcase and began pressing her with question after question. He frantically typed in notes as she answered as honestly as she could.

"I think you should know I've never acted before. Ever. No school plays—nothing," said Bree, shifting her gaze from the manager to George Kane. The fact was, she had no aspirations whatsoever of becoming an actor.

"That's a relief," grumbled the director. He stared broodingly out the dark-tinted window. "Actors can be such a pain."

Bronfmann leaned toward her and said in a low voice, "It's nothing, really. Eating, drinking, maybe a little ad-lib conversation. Just think of it as a kind of blind date. Your dinner partner will help you out." He noted the worried look on her face and gave a small chuckle. "Don't concern yourself, Miss Gaston. We're not asking for an Oscar performance. You can eat, can't you?"

"Yes," said Bree tentatively. What had she gotten herself into?

"You can drink? Answer questions? Ask questions?"

Bree shot him an odd look. "Er, yes, of course. But—"

"Well, there you go!" said Bronfmann, grinning reassuringly. "You're practically overqualified!"

The limousine sped down Roosevelt Street and abruptly

nosed into a parking lot, somehow managing to squeeze into an impossibly narrow space between two vans bearing the logo CSC. It took Bree a few seconds to figure out the letters stood for "The Camera-Shy Cupid."

George Kane stepped out, squinted up at the sun, and gave Bree a last-minute once-over. "Take her to wardrobe," he instructed.

Bree was ushered through what looked to have once been part of a kitchen scullery. Now it was painted with the BBA Production logo, and there was a mystical fastidiousness about the place that gave Bree the impression she was about to enter a whole different world, a world she suspected was even stranger and busier than the one she had just come from. Bronfmann led her through the corridor, pausing before an unmarked door on the left. He pushed it open.

An elderly woman with pins dangling from her lips was bent over, hemming a young woman's skirt. The young woman looked up and smiled. Her lacy black slip contrasted with the pallor of her skin and looked out of place with the remainder of the clothes she wore, which consisted of but a pinkish-red frilly apron and a waitress chapeau poised like a tiara on her head.

"This is Bree Gaston, the new extra. Give her something to wear," said Bronfmann. And before Bree could turn around he had already closed the door behind him.

"Hi, I'm Lori. I'll be your waitress today," the girl said with an unself-conscious wave of her hand.

"Uh, hi. Look, I've never done this type of thing—"

The wardrobe woman removed the pins from her mouth and stood with her hands on her hips, gazing at Bree. "Size five," she said, then nodded to herself as if to agree with her own assessment.

"Yes," said Bree, surprised. "But really, I've never—"

The Camera-Shy Cupid

The waitress was buttoning up her blouse. "You better get a move on. The director's kind of insane about tardiness. Last week he fired three walk-on extras for coming through the door thirty seconds after their cue." She patted Bree's arm. "Hey! Relax. The food's really not that bad." She winced a little and quickly exited.

The food? Bree patted her stomach nervously.

The wardrobe woman had already selected her outfit and was holding it up to her. "With your coloring and that hair, you should wear more pastels and greens. Try this on." She handed Bree the dress.

Bree stared at it. "Where's the rest of it?" she asked, blinking. "You want me to wear . . . this?" The dress she held up was a green Spandex number, and it was very, very small. "You sure this wasn't intended for someone a little smaller, like say . . . a mouse?"

The elderly woman draped a muslin floral scarf about Bree's neck. "Perfect," she said with a satisfied grimace. She was studying Bree's shoes. "By the way, they call me Mrs. H around here. Size eight?"

"Eight and a half," Bree corrected. "Mrs., uh, H—?"

"Haliburtestenstein. Well, you know how it is. Not enough time to spill out all those syllables, I suppose. Eleven years in this business, and nobody's ever called me by my real name. But then, most of the names floating around here are made up, aren't they?" She sighed. "Well, you'd better get a move on, dear."

"Listen, Mrs., uh, H, I've never done this sort of thing before. I mean, I'm not an . . . actor," Bree confessed.

"Here, try these on." Mrs. H set down a pair of high-heeled tan shoes in front of her. "Thank goodness you're wearing the right shade of hose, at least. You know how many pairs of stockings these people go through?"

Bree slipped her feet into the pumps. "They fit," she told Mrs. H, surprised.

The wardrobe woman nodded. "Uh-huh. You don't want to be late your first day, dear."

Bree reluctantly changed out of her own skirt and comfortable T-shirt, and tugged on the green dress.

"Everybody gets the jitters their first day. But I guarantee it'll become old hat after a while. After all, a job's a job, right?" Mrs. H adjusted the scarf around Bree's neck. "If you ever need me"—she sighed resignedly—"I'm always here. I practically live in this room."

"This dress—it's a little tight, don't you think, Mrs., er, H?" said Bree self-consciously.

"You look wonderful," said Mrs. H, smiling. She laid a reassuring hand on her arm. "Don't let little George's bark intimidate you. It's much worse than his bite, believe me."

Bree thought about what Lori the waitress had told her, about George Kane firing those three extras. She could feel the perspiration suddenly prickling under her arms.

"Makeup will be making its rounds now. You'd better hustle," said Mrs. H, steering her toward the door.

"But I don't know where—"

A man burst through the door and nearly collided with Bree. She recognized him immediately as the star of "The Camera-Shy Cupid," Grey Blaine. He pushed past Bree, barely noticing her there.

"Mrs. H! I've got a gravy stain. I need a new shirt, pronto!" he whined.

Bree scooped up her book bag with the script inside and walked stiltedly past the open door and down the corridor, pulling down the hem of her tight green dress. So tight was the Spandex material that it left her almost breathless. She suddenly felt exposed and ridiculous. *What have I gotten myself into?* she asked herself with a silent, embarassed moan.

The corridor opened onto a well-lit restaurant set where

The Camera-Shy Cupid

people sat poised over plates of food, adjusting their hair and clothes while two men and a wafer-thin woman glided from table to table with makeup palettes. Cameras were positioned like bazookas at strategic points about the room, and Bree felt herself instinctively shrinking away from them. But after a moment her shyness faded and was replaced by bewildered amazement. All around her lights dazzled in stark brightness, and a constant murmuring filtered through the place, a scene set up to look like one of those generic street-corner diners. People in headsets hastened back and forth, gesticulating code signals to one another with their hands. Back in her quiet little cubbyhole at the BBA Production building, Bree had only *read* about scenes like this.

"Bree Gaston?" A man with a clipboard suddenly appeared from nowhere. "I'm Bill—Bill from Casting," he introduced himself.

Bree shook his thin, dry hand and he led her to a table near the center of the room. A young man with a jaunty, boyish look gazed up at her and grinned.

"Bree, this is Richard Bell. Richard—Bree."

"Hi." She looked back at Bill, slightly panicked now. "Uh, I don't know what I'm supposed to—"

Bill eyed her book bag and told her he'd give it to one of the crew for safekeeping. He continued to scrutinze her. "Makeup!" he suddenly shouted to no one in particular.

Bree's hand flew to her face. Normally, she wore just a bit of mascara, maybe some lipstick. Today, she realized, she was wearing neither.

The man sitting opposite her leaned forward, his deep-blue eyes twinkling. "Some people need makeup," he said.

Bree pursed her lips, fixing him with a cool gaze. "Why, thank you," she said sarcastically.

A puzzled look flitted briefly across Richard Bell's face.

Realization of what he had said suddenly dawned on him. "Wait, no. That's not—"

"Chin up, please," said the makeup man. He took in Bree's skintight green dress and the muslin scarf, turning her face left and right. "Beautiful eyes," he muttered, and began powdering her face enthusiastically.

"I was just about to say the same thing," said Richard.

Bree shot him a frosty look. The makeup man started in on her cheeks, his hands working with practiced speed.

"I was just saying she doesn't need much makeup," added Richard.

"You do your job, I'll do mine," retorted the makeup man.

Bree's dark gray eyes itched, feeling unnaturally heavy after three colors of shadow and coat after coat of mascara were painstakingly applied. The makeup man slapped away her hand, and told her to stop blinking as he began lining her eyes with a liquid stick.

"Lips, please." He tilted up her chin, puckering his own lips.

Bree emulated him, suddenly conscious of the watchful gaze of the man seated across from her. *How did I get myself into this position? I'm not an actor, I'm a script reader!* she wailed silently.

A grip man with a light meter approached their table. He brought it up to Richard's nose, then clicked it as he swung it in Bree's direction. Richard stared at Bree. The grip read his meter, nodded, and left. Richard Bell continued to stare at Bree.

"You're staring," she said. Anxiety fluttered inside her chest, kindled now with a new sense of frustration as she gazed about her, watching crewmen with clipboards dash back and forth. *Take a deep breath, Bree,* she told herself. But with the dress Saran-Wrapped around her body, she thought deep breaths might very well rip apart the seams.

The Camera-Shy Cupid

"You look beautiful." Richard smiled at her. "But you looked better before they . . . ah—" He winced, searching for the right words.

"All right, folks!" called out a man from behind the cameras. His ripped jeans and disheveled long hair gave him the appearance of having just crawled out of bed. He yawned and scratched his head. He glanced over at George Kane, who nodded, looking bored. "All right! Quiet on the set! Restaurant scene fourteen— And . . . five, four, three . . ."

Theme music floated through the room, then faded. Bree glanced around at the other actors, her gaze lingering over the cameras and lights and the crew working behind them.

"Whoa! Look at me, not the cameras," whispered Richard. "Eat your, uh, pasta salad," he urged when Bree stared at him, puzzled.

"I thought they were supposed to say 'Action'?" she said, frowning.

"Not so loud," warned Richard in a low voice. "Is this your first time, or something?" He took a sip of his Coke. "So how did you like the concert?" he whispered.

"What concert?"

"Tone down your voice a little, okay? We're not the stars of this show, you know," he said with a frustrated smile. "Can't you ad-lib?" he mumbled almost inaudibly. "So Bree—is that an Irish name? Bree . . . what's your last name, Bree? It's not Cheese, by any chance, is it?" He chuckled at his own joke.

"What? I can't hear you," said Bree, leaning toward him, frowning.

"Just say anything," hissed Richard, his smile beginning to strain.

"What? Speak up!" Nerves made her pitch her voice

higher, and she realized from Richard's expression she'd uttered this a little too loudly.

"Cut!"

Richard shook his head as Bree watched the director approach their table. The inside of her mouth went suddenly dry as George Kane hunkered down beside her. He stroked his goatee patiently, and took her hand in both of his.

"Darling, you're holding us up," he said with a patient smile. He put his finger to his lips. Bree nodded understandingly; yes, she had to speak more softly. George Kane patted her hand and pressed his lips together. He gestured to the man in the ripped jeans and returned to his chair, positioned behind the main camera.

Countdown began again and Grey Blaine and his co-stars replayed their opening dialogue scene. Bree listened, and her eyes lit up suddenly. She recognized the script; it had passed her desk a couple of months ago. A silly little piece, but perfect for the sitcom; she had recommended it personally.

"So, Bree, what is your last name? Or is it a secret?" asked Richard, attempting to bring her attention back to where it was supposed to be.

Bree gazed at him but did not answer.

"You know, this isn't a monologue. We're supposed to be talking to *each other*," he said with an impatient sigh. "This is supposed to look *natural*."

How can I be natural, looking like this? thought Bree, tugging down the hem of her skintight dress. She shifted in her chair, trying unsuccessfully to find a comfortable position. She crossed and uncrossed her legs self-consciously, listening to another couple of extras acting behind her. She thought she heard the words "cantaloupe," and "watermelon." And indeed, after a moment

The Camera-Shy Cupid 13

she realized that these words constituted the entirety of their conversation.

Richard gestured to her food. "Mmmm . . . that pasta salad sure looks good. Cantaloupe."

Bree's brow shot up quizzically. "Cantaloupe pasta?"

"Watermelon," answered Richard, bobbing his head. He smiled and made a small gesture toward her plate.

Bree frowned and bent down, sniffing the food in front of her. She forked a noodle and wrinkled her nose. She was thinking the corkscrewed morsel looked like the entrail of a long-dead animal. She watched Richard chew on a cold french fry. Her stomach suddenly felt queasy.

"Eat. You could use some meat on those bones," Richard said softly.

Bree reluctantly popped the noodle into her mouth. It had a rubbery texture, tasting faintly of vinegar and stale soda crackers. She reached for her Coke and took a long sip from the straw. But the drink went down the wrong way and she started coughing.

"Well." He sighed. "Why don't you tell me the story of your life?" suggested Richard, wincing slightly as Bree struggled to control her choking spasm.

"Story of my life?" She gasped, clutching her throat.

"You know, you're very beautiful when you're choking," whispered Richard, grinning.

Bree glared at him and took another swallow of her drink. There was something funny about the taste, something unreal—

"It's the hair, maybe. I love red hair. The curls I can do without—ah, but it works on you. However, the dress—"

"This isn't my dress," said Bree indignantly.

"And I'd get rid of the scarf," whispered Richard, smiling. "I like to see my date's neck."

"I am not your date!"

"Low-key, remember?" Richard reminded her. "I was just making polite conversation." He gave her a wolfish grin, his eyes roaming from her head to her toes.

"Do you mind?" hissed Bree, her jaw muscles twitching.

"If you didn't want me to notice, you shouldn't have worn that dress," he said, munching on his fries.

"I told you, this is not my dress!"

Richard suddenly threw back his head and emitted a silent laugh. "Cantaloupe," he said.

"What the heck are you laughing at?" said Bree crossly. She glanced back at the couple behind them. "And what's with all this 'cantaloupe' and 'watermelon' business?"

Richard's smile stretched into a grimace. "We're supposed to be having fun," he said between gritted teeth. "We're a happy couple, after all."

"We are not a couple!" Bree's nostrils flared.

"Hey, we're on TV, remember? Extras are supposed to be seen, not heard." He rolled his eyes. "Where did they find you, anyway? The Acting School for the Unsubtle and Humorless?" he grumbled under his breath.

But Bree heard him. "Don't patronize me," she said, a little too loudly.

Richard's fist clenched and unclenched. "Look, you're not making this easy," he said, raising his own voice. "Eat your stupid pasta salad. Drink—do *something!*"

"Cut!"

Bree froze. Richard sighed, rolled his eyes, and flashed her a teeth-grinding stare.

"Is there a problem here?" George Kane stood, arms folded across his chest, staring down at Richard.

For a brief moment, Bree felt a small stab of guilt as the director glared at Richard Bell with red-faced annoyance. She had to remember that her dinner partner did this

The Camera-Shy Cupid 15

for a living; the last thing she wanted to do was cost him his job. She glanced about the set and saw the other extra actors watching them uneasily.

But her empathy, she quickly saw, was wasted on Richard Bell. He appeared neither nervous nor concerned. The powerful presence of George Kane seemed not to intimidate him in the least.

Well, what did you expect, Bree? He's an actor, she reminded herself with a derisive snort.

"Okay! Let's do it again!" yelled George Kane, throwing up his hands. And Bree could hear him muttering as he retreated back behind the scenes: ". . . ahh, the sea is beckoning to you, George. You should have been a fisherman, I tell ya. Out there with just the sea and the fish . . ."

And at the same time, Richard was grumbling: ". . . what'd you expect? Setting me up with a nightmare date. . . ."

I'll make it a nightmare for you, thought Bree. But she kept her mouth shut while the man in the ripped jeans began the countdown:

"And . . . five, four, three . . ."

Richard ate a cold french fry and swallowed. "Hey, can we call a truce? This is not a good time for me to get fired," he said softly. His smile was saccharine sweet.

Bree eyed him warily. A quick, sweeping glance told her he wasn't wearing a wedding ring. He didn't have a wife or a family to support, she surmised. How much did extra work pay, anyway? Her gaze drifted slightly left where the main scene was playing out under the cameras. Grey Blaine was performing his one-liner Buster Keaton comedy routine which he masked as acting. All of his costars, Bree now realized, were comedians as well. The only actor among them was Patti Cameron, the veteran actress who played the role of Grey Blaine's stepmother.

But what had Bree read recently in the *BBA Entertainment Monthly*? *"What actors really want to do is direct; what directors really want is to act; what comedians really want is to direct, act, produce...."*

Actors, comedians, directors: they were all the same to her. About a year ago, Bree had dated what the industry would refer to as a "rising young actor." This particular rising young actor's name was Ken Doll; what his real name was, Bree never did find out. And she never stuck around to find out.

They'd gone out to one of those chic restaurants that movie and television stars and important producer executives were rumored to frequent (a rumor usually started by the restaurant owners themselves). Of course, none of these influential people showed up, but Ken Doll still spent the entire evening talking to her out of the side of his mouth, his perfect green eyes wandering from table to table, in hopes, she supposed, that he might suddenly be "discovered."

He'd taken her then to see a Biff Smythe movie, one of those blood-spewing, chew-'em-up, spit-'em-out films Bree hated. And afterward, they sat in an overcrowded coffee shop discussing the movie (what little there was to discuss). For little over an hour, Ken Doll methodically proceeded to cut up the film, pointing out places in scenes, where he, the "rising young actor," would have performed differently, and of course, with much more effect.

Ken Doll was feeling extra confident those days; not two weeks ago he'd landed a bit part playing a young intern on a daytime soap. And, naturally, being the professional actor he was, Ken researched his role thoroughly. Figuring he knew just about all there was to know about medicine, he then decided that he had enough expertise to demonstrate his learned technique on Bree.

The Camera-Shy Cupid   17

Needless to say, the evening ended rather abruptly, with Bree hailing a cab home alone.

The last she'd heard, Ken Doll was auditioning for one of those restaurant-murder-mystery shows. His medical role on the soap opera had apparently been cut two days after their date.

What would Ken Doll think if he knew I was here? Acting as an extra on television? Bree let loose a low chuckle, and shook her head.

"What's so funny?" asked Richard, also letting loose a low chuckle.

Bree glanced at him, suddenly startled out of her reverie. "What?"

"What are you laughing at? Are you laughing at me?"

Bree rolled her eyes. "Quit being so paranoid. What are you so worried about? I don't even know you."

"But then," said Richard, his voice suddenly husky as he reached over to clasp her hand, "you're supposed to *act* like you know me. Romantically," he added, waggling his eyebrows teasingly.

Bree pulled her hand away and glared at him through narrowed eyes, her lips curling slightly. "Just keep your hands to yourself!" she hissed between her teeth.

"Suit yourself," said Richard, making certain now that Bree was not mistaking his blatant wolfish ogling for something friendly and polite. "But what's a guy supposed to think? It's hard to believe that sweet innocent act when you're dressed like that. *Women,*" he grunted. "Cantaloupe, watermelon." He grinned at her, even more infuriatingly than before.

"You—you male chauvinist pig!" And she realized, too late, she wasn't whispering anymore.

Richard exhaled loudly, grimacing, and Bree noticed then the silence that erupted about them. She turned to meet the gazes of the other extras seated about them, the crewmen's faces regarding them from behind the cameras and glaring lights. Bree flushed with embarrassment, but when she swiveled her attention briefly back to Richard, she noted his lopsided grin and the playful twinkle in his eye. Bree felt anger and indignation swell and pound like a hammer in her chest.

Make me into a fool, will you? she thought, grinding her teeth.

"I don't think I like you!" she rasped.

Richard laughed, but his deep blue eyes leveled on hers, studying her now with faint interest.

Bree braced herself for the bawling out from George Kane—perhaps even to be fired right then and there, in front of everyone. But the director remained where he was, and above Grey Blaine's nasal complaints, Bree detected a faint murmuring wafting up from behind the main camera. Everyone else on the set, it seemed, was silently waiting for the director's cue, as if caught in the middle of a game of frozen tag.

While the director spoke, fingering his goatee thoughtfully, Bronfmann glanced over at Bree and Richard. A quizzical look spread across his face. But then he nodded as if to affirm what the director was telling him. He fished his miniature laptop from his briefcase, and began keying in notes as George Kane spoke.

"Well, there goes my television career," Richard muttered, stuffing french fries into his mouth. He struck a suffering pose. "At least I got to eat today. You going to finish that pasta salad?" he asked, eyeing the plate in front of her.

Bree snorted. "I don't think you have to worry," she said. "It doesn't look like he's coming over here."

"Oh," said Richard cheerfully, "I'm not worried. It was your fault, anyway."

Bree was about to retort when the man with the ripped

The Camera-Shy Cupid

jeans announced they were starting another countdown. "Listen up, people! We're going to wrap up this scene"— he glanced over at Bree and Richard—"hopefully in this final take." He exhaled, running his fingers through his long, thinning hair. "And then you can all go home." He gestured to the cameras. "And . . . five, four, three . . ."

"Ah . . . now I see," said Richard with a smug grin.

"See what?" said Bree, staring down at the plate of cold pasta. Her stomach rumbled. She quickly pressed the heel of her hand to her abdomen, but the noise seemed to roll out of her like thunder. When was the last time she'd eaten? A quick bite of a stale Danish this morning.

"What time is it?" she asked suddenly.

Richard glanced at his watch. Bree couldn't help but notice the Mickey Mouse ears, the oversized Mickey Mouse hands pointing to the large black numbers painted on the watch face. She recognized Goofy's face etched in along the wristband. She looked at Richard, the corner of her mouth quirking up in faint amusement.

"Uh, it's almost four," Richard told her. "You have to be somewhere?" His eyebrows shot up. "You have a date with our esteemed director, perhaps? Or maybe it's one of those producers over there?"

"Huh? What—? No! Of course not! What are you implying?" she said haughtily, although she knew by his tone and the expression on his face exactly what he was implying. Why did this man insist on trying to taunt her? More to the point, why was she letting him? Anyone would think that she actually cared what he thought about her.

"I was just wondering how you actually landed this job," he said.

He gazed up at her from beneath long dark lashes. His eyes, Bree remarked, were a deep blue, not vacuous like some of the actors she'd met, but interesting, intelligent. . . .

"I'm not an actor," she replied primly.

"Well, you could have fooled me." But there was no hint of sarcasm in his voice. "I think you made quite an impression on those bigwig executives standing over there. Hold it! Don't look over. Just keep staring at me—as if you're absolutely fascinated by our conversation. Pretend. . . . pretend you're in love with me."

Bree fought down the blush that was creeping into her face. "That might prove to be a little difficult," she managed to grumble under her breath. But she didn't avert her eyes. Richard reached across the table and slid his hand under hers. Immediately, she started to withdraw, but he clasped her fingers tightly before she could snatch her hand away.

"Take it easy. I just want to read your palm—see if you're the kind of person you claim to be."

Bree regarded him skeptically. "You read palms?"

She twitched a little as he gently traced the lines of her palm, pausing over the callus on her middle finger.

"Hold still." His lips parted in concentration, and when he gazed up at her, Bree saw the blue of his eyes had darkened, and that small beads of sweat had gathered at his temples. A rush of heat washed through her suddenly and she pulled her lips into a faint smile.

"Okay, that's enough," she said, pulling her hand away.

"Hmmm . . . cantaloupe," he muttered slowly. "Elephant shoes."

"Elephant shoes?" She felt a moment of irritation. Or was it disappointment? "Elephant shoes?" That was all he had to say? She snuck a quick look at her dinner partner. A preoccupied, pensive expression had broken over his boyishly attractive face. What was he thinking? she wondered. And for a small instant, he had her believing he was more than just a handsome, charming actor. She shook her head, frowning.

What are you thinking, you dimwit? she berated herself. He's *acting.*

Bree sighed. "Watermelon."

Richard's brows drew together. An unreadable emotion flitted briefly across his face. "Now you're getting the hang of it," he said. But somehow the statement sounded to Bree more like an insult than a commendation.

"What I don't get is why someone would pay you to just recite the names of fruit." And at that very moment, she heard the woman muttering behind her, "Cantaloupe, watermelon, oh, yes... cantaloupe..." as if it were some religious fruit-worshipping mantra, a secret code for extra actors. Or maybe the woman was just memorizing her grocery list. Bree let out an involuntary giggle.

"Well, then, if you don't like fruit, then why don't you say something interesting, like 'elephant shoes'?"

Bree snorted. "Elephant shoes. Now where'd you come up with *that,* I wonder?" She shook her head. "It doesn't mean anything—'elephant shoes,' does it? You know, I'd love to see the faces of television viewers who actually read lips."

Richard chuckled softly. "Well, at least we give them something interesting to listen to." He tapped his chin thoughtfully. "I bet I can guess what you do for a living—that is, when you're not on a sitcom set and pretending to be in love with me."

Bree cocked an eyebrow. "Oh? I bet you can't—"

They were interrupted by the sound of theme music that seemed to float in from nowhere, surrounding them like an unforeseen fog. From behind the scenes there came a hurried shout:

"Cut! And that's a wra-ap, folks!"

Chapter Two

"All right, everyone! Go home!" The man in the ripped jeans stretched and rubbed his unshaven face with a thankful sigh. He turned languidly about, his day finished, and strolled out through the front exit. A man with a clipboard hurried after him, waving a pen frantically in the air.

And then it was as if some bomb of activity had been detonated. A flurry of movement erupted about Bree: cameramen and lighting grips hastily shut down and packed away their equipment, soundmen quietly folded up their headsets, men and women with clipboards darted about the restaurant set, herding the actors toward the exit. Voices melded and crescendoed, then slowly trickled and ebbed into distant sounds from the outside car lot. One by one the lights in the room winked out.

Bree stood watching all this, uncertain what she was supposed to be doing.

"Do you need a ride somewhere?"

The Camera-Shy Cupid   23

She spun around, momentarily lost in the swarm of activity. "Uh, I—where—?"

"Richie!" A woman with startling white teeth and bleached blond hair draped her arms possessively around Richard Bell's neck. She kissed him soundly on the lips. "Hey, we're all going to Cantonelli's." She noticed Bree then, and with a cursory sweep of her eyes, took in Bree's tight green dress and high-heeled shoes. "Oh, hi." A guarded look crept slowly into those stunning aquamarine eyes.

"Sandy Masterson, this is Bree, uh—?" Richard scratched the side of his mouth, realizing he never did actually find out her last name.

"You're welcome to join us, if you like," said Sandy. But her taut expression and tone of voice belied an obvious wariness, a subtle female territoriality that Bree sensed immediately.

"No, that's all right. I, uh, have to get back." She glanced around, searching for her book bag.

"Back where?" asked Richard, ignoring Sandy's insistent tug on his arm.

"Uh, where's my bag?"

"Bree Gaston?" A man she recognized as Bill from Casting held out a clipboard to her. He handed her a pen. "Sign here at the bottom—just at the X, please."

Bree stared at it, then looked at Bill in bewilderment. "I-I'm not really an actor. I—"

"I've been authorized to offer you a permanent extra position on 'The Camera-Shy Cupid,' Miss Gaston," he said, smiling patiently. "If you'll just sign this, please."

"But—"

"Come on, Richie." Sandy linked her arm in his and led him toward the front door.

"See you on the set, dinner partner!" Richard called out with a cheery wave.

"Miss Gaston? I'm sorry to rush you—"

"But I'm a script reader," said Bree. "I work in the BBA script department—"

"Yes, yes. We've already contacted them, Miss Gaston," said Bill, his smile wearing thin. "This is only a standard seasonal contract," he reassured her. "You'll get a call about shooting schedules this week. And the production manager likes the extras to come in a half hour early if possible."

Bree glanced briefly at the contract. The dollar figure, scrawled hastily in pen and initialed twice in the margin, immediately jumped out at her: seven hundred and fifty dollars? A week?

"This is standard?"

Bill shrugged. "The producers authorized your contract personally."

After a moment's hesitation, Bree signed her name at the bottom. Seven hundred and fifty dollars was almost a third more than what she was getting at the reading department. And she could most definitely use the money.

She'd just about given up hope on her old green Rabbit, which had been sitting in her apartment parking space for over two months now. After looking the car over, however, her friend Zachary advised her to junk it. According to him, the car needed an entire engine overhaul—not to mention new brake pads and taillights. The tally of repairs could easily afford her a brand-new car. So, wouldn't it be more prudent to invest in a *new* car? Zachary suggested.

But Bree had grown attached to that old car, as she did with so many other of her things. Sentimentality and a strong sense of loyalty would not allow her to consider getting rid of it. The Rabbit had been, after all, her very first car, and it had served her well for the past seven years. No, she would take the extra money and reinvest it in that which she loved. And she did love that old green car.

And with the remainder of the money—well, she had some outstanding debts she really needed to deal with....

"Uh, my bag." Bree snapped out of her thoughts. "I gave it to you before—"

"It's over there." Bill pointed to the corner of the restaurant set where a woman in gray coveralls was mopping.

CSC CLEANUP CREW was embroidered across the back.

"Thanks. When do I—?" But Bill was dashing across the room, catching up with another extra before the actor slipped through the exit doorway.

Bree started toward the service woman, and stumbled, her right foot slipping out from beneath her. She regained her balance, wincing and cursing the high, thin heels of her shoes. The tight green dress hiked up her thighs as she walked, and Bree hastily tugged it down. Like a penguin, she shambled to the corner of the room, and as the woman moved leftward with her mop, Bree spied her bag. She bent her knees, her back rigid, and managed to scoop it up without tearing anything.

"Well, hi again," said the service woman.

Bree gazed at the woman blankly.

"Lori? Lori the waitress? We met earlier in the wardrobe room."

"Oh," said Bree. "I, uh, didn't recognize you. I thought you worked as, uh, an extra on this set."

"I've been filling in for the extra who got fired last season," said Lori. "They said it was because she spilled hot tea on Grey Blaine, but I was there—and everyone pretty much knew that she and Grey Blaine were an item—at least until he dumped her, that is. She did it on purpose, I think. Of course, it got her fired, and, well...

I just happened to be at the right place at the right time, I guess." Lori grinned.

"Sounds familiar," muttered Bree.

"I think you were a hit today. Your name's Bree, right? Bree Gaston?" she went on, not bothering to wait for Bree's response, and her voice suddenly softened into a whisper. "I happened to overhear Cromwell and Penny Dowling talking about you."

"Me?" Charles Cromwell was a producer on "The Camera-Shy Cupid."

Bree recalled seeing his name on the script producers' listing. "Who is Penny Dowling?" she asked.

Lori's brows shot up. "Penny Dowling? You know, she used to play Little Gabby, from that TV show 'Stylin'?" She nodded at the sudden recognition that lit up Bree's expression.

"Yes, well, anyway, I heard she's directing commercials now, or something." Lori leaned on her mop and surveyed Bree's outfit with a curious eye. "You're lucky you fit into that dress. Don't worry, Mrs. H is pretty good about wardrobe loans. I once forgot to return that stupid waitress hat and rode the bus all the way home with it on. No wonder I was getting the looks I was getting." She laughed.

"Actually, I was just going to go change into my regular clothes," said Bree.

Lori frowned. "Mrs. H has already gone home."

I thought she practically lived in that room. "Well, the wardrobe room is still open, right? My clothes are still in there."

Lori shook her head. "They lock up all the equipment rooms." A low moan gurgled up from Bree's throat. "You wouldn't happen to have a key, would you?" She glanced anxiously about the set. Another man in gray cov-

The Camera-Shy Cupid 27

eralls was moving from table to table scraping uneaten food from the plates into a large green garbage bag.

"The security guard's shift starts at eight. You're welcome to wait, if you like."

The thought of hanging around this place for three more hours did not exactly enthrall her. With the lights turned low, and the abandoned equipment lurking tall and suspiciously silent in the shadowed corners, the restaurant set was suddenly transformed into one of those creepy haunted houses worthy of the great Vincent Price. It reminded Bree of a particularly gruesome scene in one of the scripts she'd read for "Sting Like a Bee." Though ultimately she had not recommended the teleplay, it had, nonetheless, left an impression on her (perhaps because it was that bad).

She suddenly remembered, then, the script she'd shoved into her bag. It was against BBA regulations to remove script submissions from the reading department. But she still had time to get it back over to Zachary's office.

"Is there a phone in here?"

"Yeah, in the security booth, but that's locked, too. We're supposed to use the pay phone outside."

What kind of place was this? thought Bree, annoyed. But she supposed they couldn't very well have phones ringing during shooting, interrupting the scenes. She thanked Lori, and shuffled in her high heels carefully toward the front exit. She reached her hand around and yanked down the short hem of her dress, holding it there as she walked.

Outside, she located the pay phone at the far east end of the building. She searched through her bag for her wallet, retrieved it, and found that she had exactly four single dollar bills, a nickle, and three pennies.

As she scoured the bottom of her bag for loose change,

the strap slipped off her shoulder and fell, spilling its contents onto the asphalt. "Darn!"

In that moment a cloud scudded across the sun, and a gust of wind gathered and whisked down through the parking lot. With a quick movement of her foot, Bree stopped a now-bruised apple from rolling into the gutter, her other heel stepping on the sheaf of papers that threatened to blow away.

"Oh yes. Thank you, Mr. Breeze-Coming-Out-From-Nowhere," she grumbled. All day it had been a clear, mild 21 degrees. Now wispy clouds invaded the blue of the sky. They blotted out the warm sun, causing the temperature to drop all of a sudden. Goose bumps appeared on her arms as a brisk, chill wind lifted her curls.

"Need some help?"

Bree turned her head and caught Richard Bell's amused grin. She realized with embarassment the awkward, straddled position she'd managed to maneuver herself into. As she started to bend down to pick up the script under her left foot, she remembered the dress. She silently cursed Mrs. H, the wind, her uncanny clumsiness, and Richard Bell's incredibly bad sense of timing.

Before she could say anything, Richard had picked up her book bag and was collecting the runaway pens rolling toward the grate. He threw the apple in the bag, then reached down and closed his fingers about her slender ankle. He gently lifted her heel and slid out the script.

"Oh-ho! What's this? You writing your own script, are you?" But his grin quickly faded. He frowned as he read the title page. " 'A Bird in the Hand' by Rudolph Gotham. Hmm . . . is that your pen name?" he asked.

Bree snatched it from him. "It's a pen name, all right. But it's not mine," she answered, her gray eyes flashing. For some reason she felt uncharacteristically skittish, ag-

The Camera-Shy Cupid 29

itated by this man's sudden untimely (or timely?) appearance.

"Pretty bad, is it? I guess they turned the script down then, did they?" Richard smiled in sympathy.

"This is not my script," Bree repeated. "But if you must know, it wasn't turned down. No, this script is brilliant. In fact, I might go so far as to say it's the best I've read in a long time," said Bree, jamming the script into her bag. Out of the corner of her eye she saw her handwritten recommendation fluttering across the lot.

Richard followed her gaze and lunged after it. He picked it up, paused to scan it, then began to read her written words with elevated brows, his lips quirking up in an amused grin.

"This is your recommendation?" he said, more as a statement rather than a question. He looked up from the paper. "You're a script reader."

"And you must be Sherlock Holmes." Bree tore the recommendation from his hands, annoyed.

"Writers must love you. I bet you're the kind of person who recommends everything that passes across your desk. You want to be fair—not ruffle any sensitive writer's feathers, right?"

"Wrong. Ninety percent of the scripts I read are garbage," said Bree. "But this guy—Rudolph Gotham—well, I think he'll make himself a name in the television writing business."

Richard snorted, but her impassioned tone cut short his retort. He stared at her curiously, his lips playing into a small smile.

"If, indeed, Rudolph Gotham is his real name," she added, speaking as if to herself.

"Scriptwriters usually use pseudonyms, then?"

Bree shrugged. She really shouldn't be discussing this;

if it got out that she had taken a script from the reading department—

"You waiting for someone?" asked Richard. He glanced about the empty parking lot. "I could give you a ride."

"Actually, I was going to call a cab. Uh, you wouldn't happen to have change for the phone?"

Richard patted his leather jacket pockets. "Nope. Don't carry cash on me."

Bree rolled her eyes. "My mother warned me not to accept rides from strangers."

"Hey, we're not strangers. We're in love, remember? You and I will be dining together for the next few weeks, so we might as well get to know one another, right? Oh, by the way, did they tell you about the 'Sting Like a Bee' episode? You and I are going to a cocktail party." A mischievous glint appeared in his blue eyes, and he grinned. "As a romantic couple, of course."

"No, they didn't tell me." She frowned; this whole acting thing was getting out of hand.

She gazed at the man in front of her, his unveiled amusement manifesting itself in the boyish twinkle of his blue, blue eyes, and in the wry curve of his lips. But the way he held himself—his shoulders squared, the strong chin thrust slightly forward—this showed him to be a man not short of any self-confidence. She could see, too, that he was opinionated, maybe a little too cocky for his own good. She recalled earlier how he had maintained his composure, barely blinking an eye under the angry scrutiny of George Kane. And yes, he certainly was attractive—

"I thought you had a date," she said, surprised at her sudden curtness.

"I was ambushed by Bill on my way out. He told me to look out for you," he answered.

Look out for me? She felt her cheeks suddenly grow

The Camera-Shy Cupid 31

hot with indignation. "I can take care of myself, thank you."

"Oh, really?" He cocked an eyebrow, his eyes roaming over her tight, uncomfortable attire. "Wearing that getup, I don't doubt you can take care of yourself," he mocked.

She prickled under his gaze.

"These aren't my clothes—"

"Look, we can stand here all day discussing your wardrobe, spitting out witty repartees at each other. Or I can take you home. So which will it be? I've got plenty of time," he said, folding his arms across his chest.

Bree opened her mouth for a quick retort, but decided with a sigh that he was right; she needed to get back to the BBA Production building before Zachary left for the day.

"Okay," she relented. She swept a cursory gaze over the few remaining cars parked in the lot. "Where's your car?"

"My ride's 'round back." He glanced down at her high heels. "Do you, er, need help walking?"

He did not bother to conceal the amusement in his voice, and his expression made Bree purse her lips. "No, I guess not," he said, the corners of his eyes crinkling.

Bree strolled determinedly behind him, muttering under her breath as her ankles wobbled precariously against the flimsy straps of the shoes. She was resolved not to let this absurd attire bring out her unease and gaucherie. Her mind concentrated on each step, every move. While one hand gripped the hem of the green dress, the other, encumbered by her book bag, reached up to brush back the windblown curls from her eyes. Twice she stumbled blindly, nearly tripping herself and falling. She wondered idly how fashion models made it down those long runways. Her thoughts went longingly out to her gypsy skirt and T-shirt, and most of all, to her flat, comfortable shoes stashed away somewhere in the locked wardrobe room.

"Here we are."

Bree brushed her hair away from her eyes and her lips parted first in surprise, then irritation. "You didn't tell me you rode a motorcycle."

"Put this on. Don't want to bruise that pretty head of yours." He handed her a helmet.

"Uh, maybe I should just call a cab." She eyed the motorcycle uneasily.

"Hop on. Aw, don't look so worried. I'm a great driver. After all, everything I know I learned from the movies."

"The movies?"

"You've never seen *Easy Rider*? Come on, trust me."

Bree shot him a dubious look.

"So, where're we going?"

"The BBA Production building. It's on—"

"I know where it is. Get on."

Bree hesitated.

"Don't tell me you're afraid."

She glared at him. With a deep breath, she donned the helmet and straddled the seat behind him. The green dress rumpled up to the top of her thighs. She tried unsuccessfully to smooth it down.

"Wrap your arms around my waist," he instructed. "Hang on tight."

The engine suddenly roared to life, sending vibrating waves through her. The bike lurched forward and Bree's hands instinctively tightened about Richard's firm waist. The wind stung her face, but it felt good, like a brisk cool sponge, feathering away all that heavy makeup.

Richard paused at the intersecting lights on Capitol Boulevard. Bree glimpsed the flat rooftop of the production building, the Boise Broadcasting Association logo fanning out from its center like blue-and-gold peacock feathers.

"You okay?"

"Yes." But her answer stuck in her throat. In truth, the ride exhilarated her. She could smell him now as they waited for the light to turn green. A nice, leathery smell, not heavily weighted with the pungent after-shaves so many of her dates insisted on dousing themselves with.

They rode past the art gallery and slowed as Richard swung the bike into the main parking lot. He brought them to an abrupt stop before the main glass revolving doors. Bree awkwardly dismounted, aware that the hem of her dress had hiked up. Richard watched her climb off, observing with amusement her frustration at unsuccessfully trying to suppress the flush that stained her cheeks a bright pink.

"Thank you," she grumbled.

"It's Rudolph Gotham who should be thanking me," he said, winking. "See you tomorrow, darling." And he sped off.

Darling, indeed. "Cantaloupe," she said with a parting harrumph, watching him slalom through the rows of parked cars and careen onto the street with a burst of speed. She shook her head and sighed.

Think of the money, she told herself. The end of the season was only three—four?—weeks away. *Hang in there, Bree; it's just a few weeks out of your life. And after this, you'll be able to settle back into your old, comfortable existence.*

Bree drew in a deep breath, ran a quick hand over her curly red locks, and hobbled through the glass revolving doors.

"Whoa! Baby! I think you've got the wrong room." Zachary Chalmers waggled his brows admiringly.

"Cut it out, Zachary." Bree shot him a sour look, and slumped down on the couch wearily. She tugged off the high-heeled shoes and massaged her feet. "I'd like to throttle the sadist who invented these stupid things. And whoever designed this dress should be strung up."

Zachary grinned. "Personally, I like the new you."

"This is definitely not me. How'd I get roped into this in the first place?" she wailed, her head in her hands.

"Just lucky, I guess," said Zachary. "But, hey, any woman would give her left arm to be discovered by George Kane."

"Let's not blow this out of proportion. I wasn't 'discovered,' I was ambushed. Anyway, I'm just an extra," she said. "With an extremely irritating dinner partner," she added, rolling her eyes.

"Casting already contacted us. They want you for the rest of the seasonal shoots for 'The Camera-Shy-Cupid,' " said Zachary. "And I guess they were impressed by your debut because they also want to use you in some 'Sting Like a Bee' scenes."

"Hmmm . . . yes, Richard told me." Bree gently kneaded her toes, uttering a pleasurable sigh. And then a worried expression suddenly broke through her relief. "Look, Zachary, I don't want to jeopardize my job in the reading department—"

"No problem. As soon as the season's through, you're welcome to come back here," he assured her, "that is, if you still want to come back."

"Of course I'll want to come back. You know me, Zachary. I love my job here. I'm not an actor, I'm a script reader. Only no one seems to be listening to me." She suddenly remembered why she had come to see him in the first place. She reached inside her bag. "This is the reason I'm here. I wanted to give you this." She handed the script to him along with her recommendation.

The Camera-Shy Cupid

Zachary scanned the recommendation form, his expression lighting up with sudden interest. "That good, huh?"

"Better than good—maybe even too good for 'Sting Like a Bee.'"

"Rudolph Gotham. Never heard of him. You got this from the slush pile?"

Bree nodded. "The return address is a post office box here in Boise. The telephone number looks like a local service number. I'm thinking that either this guy's a professional writing under a pen name, or some guy who's just extremely protective of his privacy."

"Either way, you think this Rudolph Gotham is a pseudonym?"

"I'm pretty certain."

"Okay, I'll look it over," said Zachary, placing it on top of the stack of scripts, which seemed never to diminish in size, but grow and grow. "And it comes at a good time. 'Sting Like a Bee' could definitely use some sprucing up. Have you seen the ratings lately? Pitiful." He patted the pile with a grin. "And who knows? Maybe you'll land an extra part in this episode."

Bree groaned. "I'm surprised I wasn't fired on the spot. You should have seen me." She shook her head. "I guess I don't watch enough TV. I'd always thought the extras had scripts, you know? That the soundmen just toned down their voices." She let out a tired laugh. "You should have heard them. It was like being surrounded by grocery store clerks: 'cantaloupe,' 'watermelon,' 'elephant shoes'—"

"'Elephant shoes?'" Zachary gazed at her, confused.

"That's one of my dinner date's ad-libs." She snorted. "That guy is so . . . infuriating."

"Oh?" Zachary's brows rose, his soft brown eyes widening slightly. "Richard Bell?"

Bree glanced at her friend. "Yes, that's his name. How'd you know?"

"Well, Casting said that you would be working as part of a, er, romantic team-up. They mentioned his name," said Zachary, chewing on his lip thoughtfully. "I have a feeling that you and Richard Bell will be working together a lot in the near future." He straightened his tie. "Oh, and I heard Penny Dowling is in town."

Penny Dowling: there's that name again, thought Bree.

"She's looking for a couple to represent some kind of candy bar, or something—a commercial series." Zachary gave her a long, sly look, his lips curving into a knowing grin. "I also heard that you and Richard Bell are seriously being considered for the project."

"What? Oh, no, no—!"

"What's the big deal? This kind of stuff could really kick-start your career."

"Zachary! I'm not interested in any of that stuff. Why doesn't anybody listen to me? I am not an actor!"

He shrugged, rising from his desk. "Well, it could be that you won't be asked, anyway. And even if you are, you can always say no, right?"

"I guess." Bree reluctantly slipped her feet back into the treacherous high-heeled shoes. "But I'm telling you, if they keep making me wear these kinds of clothes, I'm quitting."

"You signed a contract. They faxed me a copy over just a half hour ago," Zachary told her. "I looked it over; it's a one-way option: theirs."

"But I can still be fired, right?" said Bree, her lips drawing tight.

Zachary slid the script and some other file folders into his briefcase. "Aw, who would fire a beautiful woman like you? Come on, let's go out and celebrate. My treat."

The Camera-Shy Cupid

Bree rubbed her belly. It responded with a hungry growl. "Okay, but I want to go home and change first."

"Whatever you want. Although, if I may say so myself, you look pretty stunning in that dress." Zachary whistled between his teeth.

Bree narrowed her eyes and gave him a black look.

Zachary rose from his chair and with his hands made an "it's-up-to-you" gesture.

They strode out, Bree shambling and teetering along unsteadily in her tight dress and heels.

"So what're you up for? Steak? Lobster?"

"Anything but pasta salad," said Bree firmly.

Chapter Three

Mrs. H fished out the green dress from the plastic bag, inspected it with one elderly gray-blue eye, and gave Bree a nod of approval. Bree had spent the entire morning washing and ironing that torture garment. From her own wardrobe she'd elected to wear a crisp white blouse and a navy skirt, and of course, her trusty old mahogany brown loafers. Mrs. H was hastily going through the dresses hung up at the back of the room, pausing intermittently to gaze back at Bree thoughtfully.

"Gee, I thought I could wear what I have on," Bree said hopefully.

Mrs. H pulled out a pale yellow cotton dress and held it up to her. At that moment a woman strolled in, and Bree recognized her as Sandy Masterson, the girl Richard Bell had introduced to her yesterday. Her aquamarine eyes flashed Bree a tepid greeting. Her brilliant smile was cool and patronizing.

"Yellow doesn't do much for her complexion," she said, eyeing the dress.

"It's a nice dress," began Bree, "but—"

"On the other hand, you can't go out there looking like a mousy receptionist, I suppose," said Sandy, her eyes scanning Bree's navy skirt and blouse.

Mrs. H rested her hand on her hip. "No, this shade of yellow is perfect for you." She wrinkled her nose at Bree's old loafers. "Might as well wear the same shoes from yesterday."

"Oh, no! Please, I—"

"And untie your hair. Such pretty locks. You don't want to hide them."

"I think she looks better with her hair up," said Sandy, fluffing up her own peroxide-bleached hair.

Mrs. H ignored her and reached up and unfastened Bree's ponytail clip. "There!" she said with an assured smile. "Such a pretty girl."

Sandy stared at her reflection in the mirror, running her hands down over her voluptuous curves. "Mrs. H, how do *I* look?"

"You might want to borrow Miss Gaston's ponytail clip," said Mrs. H sharply.

Sandy's smile wavered and she uttered a small harrumph under her breath. She turned to Bree, her smile widening, her tanned face beaming at her.

"You know, you might want to try some cream for that puffiness under your eyes," she said, tossing her hair back. She slunk out the door, a movement that was slow and silkily alluring, how Bree pictured a mermaid might move if she had legs.

Bree did not fail to notice the woman's slim stiletto heels, amazed by and envious of her confident mastery of them. Sandy Masterson exuded a brazen attractiveness that had always seemed to elude Bree. She thought herself too gangly, her legs too thin. And her job in the script department had murdered her posture, habituating her to a slight rounding of the shoulders. Over the past three years she'd grown accustomed to hunching over scripts, altogether neglecting her mother's constant niggling advice: "Shoulders back, dear!"

Now, as if her mother had just stepped into the room, she straightened. But she immediately slumped forward again as Mrs. H brought out the shoes.

"Nobody's going to see my shoes, Mrs. H," she protested.

"If it were up to me, you could wear snow boots, for all I care. But this is my job. You have to remember, Miss Gaston, I take orders from the big guns around here." She motioned heavenward with a suffering sigh, and smoothed back her silver-gray hair.

"Please, call me Bree." She took the dress with a surrendering grimace. At least this one would give her room to breathe, she thought. As for the shoes, well, she'd just have to get used to walking in heels, wouldn't she?

As she started to unbutton her blouse, the door opened again.

"Mrs. H, I need—"

Bree stared at Richard Bell. A hot blush crept into her face, and she snatched up the sundress, clutching it close.

"Ever heard of knocking first?" she said angrily.

"Sorry, didn't realize you were in here changing," he said, unapologetically. He pointed to his shirt. "I lost a button, Mrs. H."

Mrs. H, undaunted by the interruption (she'd become accustomed to people in various stages of undress roaming about her tiny wardrobe room), reached behind her for her sewing kit. She'd been in this business too long

The Camera-Shy Cupid 41

to recognize or acknowledge modesty in the people she worked with.

"Do you mind?" Bree glowered at her dinner partner.

"No, go right ahead," he answered, grinning.

"Could you *please* turn around?" Bree's jaw clenched in frustration. She eyed the door anxiously.

Richard turned around while Mrs. H searched for a matching button.

"I bet Mrs. H here enjoys dressing you up. The clothes in this place have been hanging here for centuries—Ow!" Richard chuckled as Mrs. H gave him a dour look. "Months, I mean," he quickly amended. "I really didn't mean to barge in on you like this. Usually, our esteemed wardrobe lady is only asked to fix buttons and zippers and wash out food stains. Isn't that right, Mrs. H?"

"If people would only take the time to care for their clothes, my job would be a lot easier. Rush, rush, rush. Everyone's always in such a hurry," grunted Mrs. H. "Hold still. My goodness, when was the last time you washed this shirt? You've developed a nasty ring around the collar, young man."

Richard looked down at his collar. "So, why don't you finally quit this crazy job and marry me? You could change your name to Mrs. B," said Richard jokingly.

"No, thank you. This job is wearing me down as it is. Doing your laundry will just about break me, I think," replied Mrs. H gruffly. But beneath the harshness of her reply, Bree could hear—as she had heard in Richard's joking manner—a note of genuine affection.

Bree had by this time slipped on the sundress. She was adjusting the snug-fitting bodice when Richard turned around.

"Well, that color does suit you," said Mrs. H. She squinted at her, oblivious of Bree's embarrassment. "Isn't she a lovely girl, Richard?"

"Very," he agreed, the corners of his mouth turning up slightly.

Bree struggled ineffectively to supress the blush that stained her cheeks a bright rosy hue.

"Remember, we have a date in ten minutes," said Richard. He blew her a phantom kiss before he exited.

"Don't mind him. Deep down he's really a very nice boy."

Bree smoothed the dress. "He—he bothers me," she said, frowning.

"All the good ones do, honey." Mrs. H gazed at her thoughtfully, her small pointed features drawing into an unreadable expression. "You should wear more color. Perhaps you'd like to borrow some of the clothes in here."

She sighed. "What Richard said was true. There was a time when I outfitted everyone who came in here. That was my job. But nowadays, people already know what looks good on television. They buy their own clothes. They have no need for these anymore." She gestured toward the racks of clothes. "It seems I've become less the wardrobe lady and more an on-the-spot seamstress."

Bree nodded and smiled. "Well, you can be my wardrobe lady anytime." She grimaced as she slipped her feet into the high-heeled shoes. "But Mrs. H, couldn't you maybe find some, uh, more comfortable shoes?"

"I'll work on it." A new twinkle came into the elderly lady's keen blue-gray eyes.

"You should flag down the waitress, and order something else," said Richard in a low voice.

Bree gazed at him, not certain whether he was being ironic or serious. But really, this pasta salad was nauseating to look at: the rubbery texture of the coiled noodles and the blobs of mayonnaise haphazardly thrown in re-

The Camera-Shy Cupid

minded Bree of some traditional Klingon repast direct off the set of "Star Trek." "This is supposed to be earth food," she muttered to herself as she prodded a hard green chunk, which she had determined, out of a process of elimination, to most likely be celery.

"You know there's something wrong when you suddenly become frightened of your food," she grumbled, stifling a shudder.

"Want a bite of my burger? Sharing food is supposed to be romantic."

Bree lifted an eyebrow and gazed at her partner's meal. She swallowed down her rising hunger. Oh, why hadn't she taken time out to eat lunch?

"Here. Have a fry. They're nice and hot today." He held up a french fry. Bree reached out to take it, but he withdrew his hand. "Uh-uh. Let me feed you. Open wide."

"I will not!"

"Your mouth says no, but your belly says yes, yes, yes," said Richard, grinning, dangling the french fry teasingly.

Bree glanced around the set, and saw Lori pouring a round of coffees at the booth next to where Grey Blaine and the other stars of "The Camera-Shy Cupid" were playing out their scene. As Lori turned around, Bree waved her hand in the air to get her attention. Lori furrowed her brow uncomprehending, uncertain. She glanced briefly back at the cameras behind the scene, then, shrugging, she wended her way through the tables to Bree and Richard.

"What is it?" she whispered.

"Lori, do you think you could bring me something—"

"Cut!"

Bree winced. Richard bowed his head, and she shot him

an apologetic look. But her expression rapidly changed, with her gray eyes narrowing and glaring at him contemptuously as she saw that he was, in fact, attempting to stifle a laugh.

Lori turned to meet the red-faced George Kane, cringing before those dark button-like eyes. "Oh, I'm—"

"What in heaven's name do you think you're doing?" sputtered the director.

"I'm sorry, Mr. Kane. I—"

"It's my fault," Bree jumped in. She hadn't meant to get Lori into trouble. "It-it's just that this food is, well..." she stammered, noticing Richard was pressing his hand to his mouth, a suppressed snicker gleaming in his blue eyes.

"You're interrupting the scene, Miss Gaston," said George Kane, emphasizing each word slowly, with painstaking patience. He blinked, grimaced, and stroked his goatee.

"I was wondering if Lori might be able to bring me something—"

The vein in the director's temple throbbed dangerously. "You've been hired on as an extra, not a food critic. I don't care if you don't like the food. You're supposed to be an actor, so here's a suggestion: Why don't you *act* like you're enjoying your meal?"

He gestured to the man behind the camera and steered Lori back to her previous position at the booth. Grey Blaine beckoned him over and they exchanged a few words. The comedy star shook his head angrily, and Bree looked away when he pointed in her direction.

"Your second day on the job and already you're making waves," said Richard, leaning forward. "You're blowing our audition, you know."

"Audition?"

The Camera-Shy Cupid

"Perhaps you haven't noticed, but there are some important people watching us."

Bree gazed at him quizzically. "What? What people?"

"You don't recognize Penny Dowling over there? She was here yesterday, too, but this time it looks like she's brought along some big hotshot advertising executives. Your agent didn't tell you?"

"I don't have an agent."

"Figures," mumbled Richard, shaking his head. "Look, can't you at least make believe you're in love with me?"

"Quiet on the set!" shouted the man in the ripped jeans. Today he wore a rumpled T-shirt that read *Photographers Do It Negatively*.

"And . . . five, four, three . . ."

Richard watched Bree pick up her fork and regard the plate of cold pasta distastefully.

"Here, have a bite of my burger." Richard extended it to her. "Oh, go on. I don't have any cooties."

She looked at it, looked up at her dinner partner, then with a long-suffering sigh, she let him hold it while she took a bite. It churned in her mouth like sawdust.

"See? You thought I was better off. But really, I was only *acting*," Richard pointed out in a low voice.

Bree grabbed her Coke and took a large gulp, washing down the chalky taste of the burger. She stared at her drink. "This isn't Coke."

"Yeah, it's some cheap mock pop they always use. I heard they're not allowed to actually use brand-name drinks on the set. Everything here alludes to real food—but then, you can't believe everything you see on television, right?" He caught her pensive look. "The quality stuff must be camera shy." He chuckled silently at his own witty play on words.

"Very punny," she uttered snarkily. She snuck a sidelong glance at the couple seated at the table next to them. They drank and ate and murmured intermittently "cantaloupe" and "watermelon," playing out an unnatural display, as if it were the most natural thing in the world. Out of the corner of her eye, Bree spied Sandy Masterson, beaming like a healthy Barbie doll, her legs crossed sophisticatedly as she feigned a wide, toothy smile. Her partner, a ponytailed, peroxided version of Sandy, returned the smile, then laughed silently. But his expression hinted at boredom, his plastic smile seeming too desperate and forced.

"If you like, you can just say 'cantaloupe' or 'watermelon,' " said Richard. The blue in his eyes shone, the deep color calling to mind magazine pictures she'd seen of the Mediterranean Sea. "Or 'elephant shoes.' I don't mind."

Bree rolled her lips between her teeth, suddenly feeling ill at ease. Self-consciously she twirled a curl of hair around her finger, forcing a smile on her face. But instantly it splayed into a moody grimace.

"I can't do it," she muttered. "All this smiling, and nobody really talking. It—it just seems so silly to throw names of fruit at each other."

"We could do vegetables, if you like," suggested Richard wanly. "Or animals, plants, furniture; we could recite rude poetry, call people names behind their backs."

Bree giggled.

"Why don't you tell me your life story? We've got two whole weeks to get to know each other."

Bree rolled her eyes. "My life story? That'll take all of two minutes."

"Now, *that* I don't believe," said Richard. He reached for her hand, and before Bree could protest he turned it over and studied the lines in her palm. He nodded, an earnestness spreading into his features. "Hmmm...a

The Camera-Shy Cupid 47

long lifeline, yes—and here . . ." He traced a long horizontal wrinkle. ". . . is your love line. Interesting . . ."

"Interesting? What's so interesting?" she blurted out, unthinking. Realizing she'd inadvertently dropped her guard, revealing her piqued curiosity, Bree quickly masked it with a look of nonchalance. "Uh-huh. So what do you see, Nostradamus?" she said coolly.

Richard raised his brows, his lips playing into a teasing smile. "I see a passionate romance in your near future. But you must let yourself go, drop the cool facade, follow your heart—"

Bree gave a cynical harrumph.

"Your past, I see"—he frowned, cradling her hand firmly and drawing it closer—"was filled with fruitless relationships that obviously didn't mean anything to you."

His "fruitless" remark brought an involuntary grin to Bree's face.

"Such a pretty, interesting hand." And he bowed his head and kissed it.

Bree snatched her hand back, the clumsy reaction causing her to knock over her drink. It fell onto the floor with a loud *ping-clack!*, the dark mock pop sloshing across to the next table. Bree froze in a moment of horror, her hands flying to her mouth.

"Ack! All over my good shoes!" an extra spit out.

Bree turned to gaze into the face of a well-groomed man whose sculpted features struggled to maintain a good-humored composure. But the hazel-brown eyes flashed angrily at her.

"I'm so sorry—"

"Cut!" A low murmur hushed about the set.

Bree saw the anger in the extra's eyes metamorphose into fright.

The man in the ripped jeans clasped his hands together. "Cleanup crew!"

Bree and Richard exchanged wincing glances. But George Kane remained seated in his chair, an expression of weary defeat and exasperation stamped across his face. No doubt he was visualizing those ten-foot waves, his trusty fishing reel in hand, drinking cheap brandy with his foul-smelling mates—all that "manly Hemingway stuff," thought Bree, sighing. She didn't blame him; at that moment she was wishing she was back at her little cubbyhole desk, her feet up, coffee at hand, leisurely reading through the scripts from her slush pile.

She thought briefly about Rudolph Gotham, her recent talent discovery. Who was he? Would she ever get to meet him? she wondered. There was something about writers that attracted her—and this one especially. Perhaps it was because of the man's choice to remain anonymous. Modesty was a rare quality when it came to the business of television.

Behind the cameras and lights Bree saw Penny Dowling lean over and say a few words to the director, then turn to her left and whisper something in the ear of another man garbed in an expensive black serge suit. The man nodded and cupped his chin thoughtfully. Bree recognized Charles Cromwell standing next to him. Cromwell put his hand on the man's shoulder and uttered a few deferential words and gestures. An executive Bree knew to be Gail Sussman approached from the other side of the room, and Penny Dowling promptly rose from her chair. They stepped away from the executive group and spoke in private. Neither one seemed overly upset, but Bree couldn't be wholly certain; the scene, played out in a matter of minutes, had a surreptitious air about it—as if Bree had just witnessed some secret television producers' version of the game Telephone.

The Camera-Shy Cupid 49

A woman dressed in gray coveralls mopped up the spilled drink, and Lori approached their table with another cup, the plastic made to look like glass, bearing more dark mock pop. She winked at Bree.

"Don't worry. Last week I dropped the coffeepot. Thank goodness everything's plastic around here, but you should've seen it bounce. Boing! Right up into this guy's lap. Remember that, Richie? I thought I'd be booted out right then and there."

"Personally, I thought it added a little 'splash' to the scene." Richard grinned. "Aw, they know you're too good a waitress to lose, Lori."

Lori sighed and adjusted her frilly waitress cap. She gazed down at Bree's uneaten pasta. "Well, at least I don't have to eat in this place. Pretty gross stuff, eh?" She glanced over at the cameras and hunkered down, whispering, "Some of the extras, like Sandy Masterson over there? See how she's smiling? That's because she brings her own food—rabbit food, of course." Lori smirked a little.

A makeup man rushed over to their table, holding his palette like a serving tray. He pushed Lori out of the way and began dabbing at Bree's face with a powder puff. He tilted up her chin and studied her critically. Bree flinched, aware that her dinner partner was eyeing her as well. She quelled her annoyance as the makeup man deftly applied another coat of mascara.

At this rate I won't be able to keep my eyes open, she thought in frustration.

"Okay, people! Places everyone! Let's have some quiet in here!" the man in the ripped jeans shouted. He gestured to the cameraman, talking into his headset, his hand poised in the air.

"And . . . five, four, three . . ."

Richard flashed Bree a rueful smile. But there was a

hint of laughter in his eyes, and Bree compressed her lips primly.

"Sorry, partner. Couldn't help myself. If you'd just relax—"

Bree exhaled a deep breath. Why did this man frustrate her so? "Just keep your hands to yourself from now on," she snapped.

"Listen, I'll make it up to you. Have dinner with me. I promise the food will be real, and you can talk as loudly as you like."

"Cantaloupe," answered Bree.

"Is that a yes?"

"Watermelon."

"So you will have dinner with me? Great, I'll pick you up at eight."

"You don't know where I—oh, elephant shoes," she said, frowning, irritated by her sudden confusion.

Richard grinned. "At least smile when you say that."

"Potato." She forced her lips into a smile, but found that it took little effort to do so. Now, a peculiar excitement was stirring inside her chest. Richard tilted his head to the side, watching her. For a brief moment, their eyes met. Bree quickly looked away, furious at herself for blushing. *Stop it, Bree; you're acting like a schoolgirl.*

"Either you're the worst actress I've ever seen, or the best," mumbled Richard, stabbing a french fry with his fork. And in that instant Bree noticed his confident expression give way to a look of uncertainty.

Bree's sudden indecisiveness disturbed her. Her first reaction was to turn down his dinner offer, but now she found herself floundering, searching for something to say. But all that sported from her lips was a throaty "Cantaloupe."

Richard looked up from his plate, his smile not reaching his eyes. "Uh-huh. Watermelon, cantaloupe, potato—"

The Camera-Shy Cupid

He paused, emitting a partially contained growl. His eyes flickered, and he gave an almost imperceptible shake of his head. "Oh, and . . . elephant shoes." He grabbed up his hamburger and bit into it, not looking at her, but down at his plate.

After a moment Bree sighed, rounding her shoulders. "Okay," she said in a low voice.

"Okay, what?"

"Okay, you can buy me dinner." *There you go again, Bree, getting yourself into trouble. . . .* "If that's what you want," she added quickly.

Richard's blue eyes lit up. His lips curved into a wolfish grin.

"I'll go out with you—but only for dinner," said Bree, straightening.

"No . . . dessert?" His smile was smug.

Bree's eyes narrowed, her nostrils flaring slightly as she felt herself go rigid. Dessert? "Can I ask you a question?"

"Shoot. I have nothing to hide."

"How many girls on this set have you shared 'dessert' with?" But before he could answer she went on, her face flushed now with indignant anger. "Listen, I'm not one of your—"

"Cool it, will you? If you must know, yes, I've been out with a few of the women here—"

"Is Sandy Masterson one of those 'few'?"

Richard's eyebrows quirked up. "As a matter of fact, yes, we've dated a bit in the past." He grinned. "Can this be jealousy I'm hearing?"

Bree snorted. But she wondered, too, at her own outburst. What did she care whether he dated the girls on the set? And what he did with Sandy Masterson was really none of her business.

And yet, even as Bree rationalized these thoughts, she could not fathom this strange new feeling churning inside her. Surely she wasn't jealous? No, no, of course not. But then why on earth was she overreacting so?

"And what exactly did you think I meant by 'dessert,' anyway?" This time it was Richard's turn to look indignant, although he seemed more amused than anything by her reaction.

"Cut! And that's a wrap, people!" The man in the ripped jeans tore off his headset.

Richard gazed at her, and Bree bit her lip, suddenly feeling very foolish.

"All right, I'm sorry. I—"

"Bree!"

She turned to see Zachary pushing his way through the milling crowd of extras and crewman. He waved at her.

Richard rose from his chair, his gaze shifting from her to the approaching man in the gray gabardine suit. A crease appeared between his brows, then a look of stony understanding suddenly spread across his face. Bree stood up and started to say something, to explain—

"Hi, Bree." Zachary squeezed her shoulder affectionately. "I was just passing by, and I thought I'd drop in to see how things were going. I caught just the tail end, but you were magnificent." He grinned and kissed her cheek.

"Uh, Zachary Chalmers—Richard Bell," Bree introduced the two men.

Zachary extended his hand and Richard shook it, his eyes regarding the man coolly.

"So you're Bree's dinner partner. Hope she's not giving you any trouble. Bree can be quite a spitfire." Zachary laughed jokingly.

"Yes, I can see that." Richard's eyes leveled on hers, and Bree turned away to conceal the flush that crept into her face.

"Well, I thought I'd offer you a lift home, Bree. There

The Camera-Shy Cupid 53

are a few things we need to talk over," said Zachary, oblivious to Bree's sudden discomfort, and unaware that he'd interrupted their conversation. "The car's parked outside. You ready?"

Before Bree could respond, Richard nodded to them both. "Nice to have met you, Zachary." He abruptly turned and walked away.

Zachary frowned, puzzled. "Did I say something?"

Bree watched Richard stride past the tables. Sandy Masterson called to him and grabbed his arm. He smiled down at her healthy, tanned face, and put his arm around her. Together they strolled toward the exit.

Bree shrugged. "Just let me get my bag." But her smile was strained and forced. Inside her chest something fell with a heavy thump. She collected her bag, and gave her head a quick shake, as if to clear away the thoughts spinning there.

Don't get involved, she told herself.

She slipped off the high heels and pushed her toes into her old loafers with a contented sigh. Ah yes, this was where her feet belonged.

Zachary was chatting with Bill from Casting. He handed the man with the clipboard a card from his jacket pocket and shook Bill's hand.

"What was that all about?" Bree asked Zachary as they crossed the car lot. She noticed the grin on her friend's face.

The car alarm beeped, and Zachary unlocked the passenger door. He gazed at her, his soft brown eyes gleaming.

"Say hello to your agent."

Chapter Four

"But Zachary! What do I need an agent for? I'm not a *real* actor," protested Bree as she slammed the car door shut. "Lest you forget, I still work in the script department, remember? This job is only temporary." She shook her head and frowned. "And since when are you an acting agent, anyway?"

"Talent agent," he corrected her with a secretive, lopsided grin. "You didn't know me in New York. When I lived there I was a licensed agent. I was very ambitious. I represented some, well... some interesting entertainment acts," he said, easing the car out of the parking lot.

"Really? Anybody I'd know?"

"Hmmm... probably not. They were, er, quite unusual performers, actually," said Zachary hesitantly. "I had one guy who performed this ventriloquist act with a giant plastic guinea pig. It was quite, really quite... amusing." He chuckled to himself. "And then there was this Dutch

The Camera-Shy Cupid 55

woman who tap-danced in clogs to Cole Porter songs—"

"But no actors? Zachary, really, I'm not sure you—"

"Oh, I represented this one guy who did television commercials. I even helped him land a couple of roles in a local grocery advertisement. He played an apple and a pear, and a gourd, at least I think it was a gourd...." Zachary trailed off into a reflective pause. "I wonder whatever happened to him. Virgil Halwig. I tried to convince him to change his name, but he wouldn't hear of it. He was a nice little man, Virgil was. Granted, he was a little strange, but he was all right. You know what his big ambition was?" Zachary gave a small snort. "He wanted to be the next Maytag Repairman."

Bree slouched back against the seat, kneading the back of her neck. "Zachary, I don't know if I can handle this acting stuff. I don't know if I *want* to."

"Well, it looks like you've caught the attention of some important people in this business—actually, I should say you and Mr. Bell," Zachary corrected himself.

"What do you mean?" Bree sat up suddenly, her gray eyes snapping alert.

"Apparently, you and Richard Bell have what they're looking for." Zachary glanced at her, his eyebrows raised. "You know, that 'spark,' that 'electricity' between two people? And I have to admit I saw it as well, even with that small bit I saw today. You and this Richard—"

"I'm not sure what you're getting at," interrupted Bree. She was irritated by the flush that had risen to her cheeks. "Spark?" Zachary obviously didn't know what he was talking about. There was no spark between Richard and her.

"You're trying to tell me you're not, uh, attracted to this guy?"

"Who? Richard Bell? No, of course I'm not attracted to him," she answered haughtily. "He-he's not my... type." Bree stared out the window. Okay, so Richard Bell was handsome, and, well, yes, interesting and intelligent—but he was infuriating, too. That boyish charm irritated her; he wasn't serious enough for her. He was also an actor; actors tended to be too self-involved, egotistical.

"You see, the thing is," said Zachary, momentarily jarring her out of her thoughts, "you and Richard Bell have been offered another bit part on 'Sting Like a Bee.' A *speaking* part," he added, eyeing her, watching her reaction.

"A what? Oh, Zachary, no! Eating and saying 'cantaloupe' and 'elephant shoes,' yes, this I can handle. But actually speaking lines from a script? No, no! I can't do that. I can't *act*—"

"Sure you can, Bree. It's not as if you'll be playing a major role or anything. I've seen the script. You just have to check into a hotel, argue a little with Richard—"

"That won't be difficult," muttered Bree.

"And then, there's this business with Penny Dowling," said Zachary, pulling up into the driveway of her triplex building.

That name again. Bree braced herself against the dashboard. "What is Penny Dowling doing here in Boise, anyway?"

"She's looking for a couple to star in a series of candy commercials, or something," said Zachary. He licked his lips and smiled broadly. "And guess who's currently in the running for the role?"

Bree groaned. "Oh, please—please, don't tell me." She rubbed her eyes. "Doesn't this Penny Dowling realize I'm not an actress?"

Zachary shrugged. "Like I said, you and Richard Bell apparently have that special something she's looking for.

The Camera-Shy Cupid 57

And you have to admit that you and this Bell fellow, well, sparks do seem to fly when you two are together."

It was true Richard stirred something in her. But was it attraction? Her heart beat a little faster with this thought, and deep in the pit of her stomach a nervousness began to flutter. She rubbed her eyes, smearing the mauve shadow and black mascara. Gazing at her stained fingertips, she shook her head, "Zachary, I don't know about this...."

"Hey, there's only a couple of more weeks of shooting left in this year's season. And these commercials—if, in fact, you do get the job—are just a week's, maybe two weeks' worth of work," Zachary reassured her.

"And my job at the reading department?"

"It'll still be there if you choose to come back." Zachary nosed in beside her old Rabbit. "But in the meantime, why don't you just enjoy your new notoriety? Hey, some of those actors on that set have been playing bit parts for years, just waiting to be discovered. And look at you—two days on the job and already you're turning heads. Bree, this could be your big chance."

"My big chance for what? Zachary, you know I'm not an actor. This is all a big mistake." Bree sighed.

"Well, then, look at it from the money angle." He gazed over at her old green Rabbit, and wrinkled his nose as he took in the scabrous paint, the rusted door handles, the nearly bald tires. "You'll be able to fix up this old rodent junk heap of yours—or maybe even buy a brand-new one." He glanced up at the rambling, sallow-bricked triplex where she'd lived for the past three years. A scruffy bearded man dozed on the steps, nestling a bottle-shaped paper bag to his chest.

"And maybe move into a decent neighborhood," Zachary added after a moment.

"I'm happy where I am, thank you," said Bree rather

defensively. She followed Zachary's gaze to the old man sitting on the front stoop.

Mr. Braxton lived in an apartment in the basement, but Bree never actually saw him ever go into it. He was always out sitting on the front steps, like one of those homeless cats who came around to rest on the stoop and be around people. He meant no harm, and despite his slovenly appearance, Bree knew Mr. Braxton to be a decent, honest person. In fact, she found herself (as she was now) being very protective of the old man.

However, Bree had to admit she was fast growing tired of having to suffer through all the inconveniences that seemed to crop up on a regular basis (to which the landlord so lightly referred to as the building's "character"): the twenty-minute wait for six minutes of hot water; the continual breaking down of the air-conditioning system during the hottest summer months; the temperamental heating system at Christmastime; the shrieking pipes, the overflowing toilet, the creaky floors. . . . Bree sighed.

"The producers of 'Sting Like a Bee' want to rehearse you for the bit speaking part on Friday." Zachary flipped open his notepad. "They also want you for a walk-on, walk-off scene."

"What? 'Walk-on, walk-off'? When's this?"

"The day after tomorrow."

Bree exhaled loudly. "Okay, but if you're going to be my agent, I want you to talk with me first. Extra acting, yes, I think I can deal with that, but this speaking—"

"Oh, and by the way, I read that script you gave me yesterday."

"And? What'd you think?" Bree's eyes lit up.

Zachary nodded. "You were right. It's a darn good piece of writing. Production management's already approved it. They want to shoot it in the next few months." He furrowed his brow, gnawing on his lip for a moment.

"But this Rudolph Gotham is hard to get a hold of. I could only get his answering service, and he's not listed in any of the directories. We left a message and sent the contract to the post office box," he told her. "It's not really unusual, writers writing under a pen name. Some of these people just don't have any real fixed address; some are just transients. But my guess is that this guy is using the name Rudolph Gotham as a cover, to hide his real identity, which I suspect might conflict with his present employment—or status."

"You think he's already in the television business, then? Some head honcho, maybe?" Bree mused on this thought. "Or perhaps he's a well-known literary figure?"

"Or it could be that he's just a very private person. And you know, 'he' could very well be a 'she'—like George Eliot, or . . . Charles Dickens."

"Charles Dickens *was* a man!"

"Whatever. You're the literature expert," said Zachary distractedly. "In any case, we'll see what happens with the contract. Who knows? He might not even sign it. And there's always the chance that this guy's just a one-time scriptwriter who got lucky first time around. And, well, you know how this business deals with guys like that."

Bree shook her head. "I haven't come across a real talent like this in a long time. No, I-I have a good feeling about this Rudolph Gotham."

Zachary glanced sharply at his friend, his lips turning up slightly. He frowned quizzically. "Why all this sudden interest in this Rudolph guy? A guy you've never even met?"

Bree shrugged, not quite certain herself why this writer had managed to pique her interest. Maybe because recently, all her dates have been miserable disappointments. Maybe because she sensed in this particular writer an intelligence and sensitivity that she'd found lacking in most of the men she met. Hadn't she always fantasized about settling down with a writer? But the writers she'd dated up to now had been hacks, with loud, obnoxious personalities—and egos to match. She sighed resignedly; Rudolph Gotham was probably just as egotistical as the rest of them.

"You need to get out more, Bree. Date more people," said Zachary. "And it's not like you're hurting in the looks department. Listen, there's this guy Rachel knows—"

"Oh, no! No more blind dates."

"But this guy works with Rachel. I've met him. Nice-looking, and he's recently single—a divorcé, actually—"

"Oh, no. Not another divorcé," said Bree, rolling her eyes. "Remember the last divorcé you and Rachel set me up with? He spent the entire evening talking about his ex-wife like she was on 'America's Most Wanted.' " Bree pursed her lips resolutely. "No, absolutely not. I'm still trying to get over that Jimmy guy—you know, the Stan Laurel look-alike you and I and Rachel went out with? Remember? His wife ran away with the vacuum cleaner salesman? Yeah, well, I still have the tear stains on my dress from when he cried all night on my shoulder. Uh-uh. No way."

Zachary scratched his chin. "Yeah, fixing you up with Jimmy Crane might have been a bit of a mistake. But maybe if Rachel and I had you over for dinner, you could meet this guy she works with—"

"I'll think about it," said Bree noncommittally. She opened the car door.

"Oh, I forgot. You're expected on the set tomorrow at one o'clock," said Zachary. He leaned over the seat. "Just think of it as a free lunch."

Bree screwed up her face, blew out a long exhalation,

The Camera-Shy Cupid 61

and swung her legs out. She climbed out of the car wearily. "I guess I can a handle a couple more weeks of this."

"Bah! You'll change your tune when you become rich and famous." Zachary grinned.

Bree shot him a sour look as she shut the door and waved. But as she strolled up the weed-ridden path to her triplex entrance, her heart was dancing a little. In retrospect, it *was* rather nice to be noticed, to be selected out of all those other actors. But a commercial? She laughed.

But then, it wasn't just her; it was she and Richard Bell. *"Sparks do seem to fly when you two are together."* Could it be that there was some sort of invisible mutual attraction going on between her and this man?

She hastily shrugged this thought away. No, he wasn't her type. He was an actor, an entertainer. And Bree wasn't looking to get involved with someone who could act the part. She let out a sardonic snuffle; most likely he had a longer history of casual dating than Rudolph Valentino. *How many hearts has he broken?* she wondered.

Bree fit the key into her apartment lock. *No, this is one heart he's not going to have a chance to break.* She entered the apartment and nodded to herself. If he asked her out again, she'd turn him down, she told herself with a determined grimace. She recalled his twinkling blue eyes, the strong chin, remembering the way her arms wrapped around his taut waist, his manly smell—

"Bree Gaston! Richard Bell is not your type!" she said aloud to her reflection in the hall mirror. But she could see that her own eyes were not wholly convinced by this indignant proclamation. And somewhere in her chest, her heart involuntarily echoed their sentiment. She closed her eyes and tried to picture Rudolph Gotham. But the face that stared back at her was that of her infuriating "Camera-Shy Cupid" dinner partner.

"Ugh! Elephant shoes!" She stuck her tongue out at the mirror.

Chapter Five

"Watermelon," said Bree, smiling slightly.

"Cantaloupe," retorted Richard.

"Pecan pie."

"Asparagus quiche."

"Crème caramel."

"Elephant shoes," said Bree, her brows drawing together.

"Yes." Richard's eyes softened, his grin widening. "Elephant shoes."

His change in tone caught Bree off-guard. For three solid minutes, they'd been shooting edible barbs at each other, nodding and smiling politely, not allowing themselves to rise above this level of excitement. Bree had thought it kind of a game. But now his look made her flush and she realized with annoyance that she'd lost the match.

"Uh, macaroni and cheese."

"I thought you didn't like pasta."

"Strawberry shortcake."

"Or dessert." Richard cocked an amused eyebrow. "Did you and Zachary Chalmers, by chance, have... dessert last night?"

"What—?" Bree's back went rigid. The corners of her lips pulled taut, her expression indignant. "For your information—not that it's any of your business—Zachary is married."

Richard narrowed his eyes and studied her for an instant. He shook his head. "And here I thought you were a nice girl."

"Zachary is my friend," said Bree hotly. "I work with him in the script department. He's—he's a script supervisor."

"Oh, I see. You only go out with the big honchos."

"It's not like that!" She glowered at him. "Rachel and I are friends. Oh, why am I bothering to explain anything to you?"

"So does this mean you're free tonight?"

Bree glanced at him, her pulse suddenly quickening. "I—no. No, I don't think we should—"

"Well, it just so happens *I'm* free tonight," said Richard, leaning forward. "How about it?"

"How about what? Gee, you really know how to sweep a girl off her feet."

"Is that what you want? To be swept off your feet? Because there's a broom over there...."

"So," said Bree, "Sandy Masterson must be busy tonight." Her eyes sized him up warily.

"I don't know. I never asked her," said Richard, shrugging. "You like Spencer Tracy?"

"Am I the only woman here you *haven't* dated?" said Bree, moving her fork around. Pasta salad again. She struggled to keep the smile on her face, but it was difficult.

"What about Katharine Hepburn? All women like Katharine Hepburn, right?" Richard muttered this as if speaking to himself. He was staring at his plate of fries. "You see, there's this double feature playing at the Angel Cinema: *Adam's Rib* and *Woman of the Year*."

"Cantaloupe," said Bree, not daring to meet his gaze. Why was her heart pounding?

"Is that a yes?"

"Watermelon."

"Okay, I'll pick you up at seven."

Bree's eyes flickered behind her lashes. "Elephant shoes," she said. She heard the faint note of desperation behind her words. Why couldn't she just say no?

"Now, that's a definite yes if I ever heard one." Richard chuckled.

"I-I don't think it's a good idea," said Bree, glancing up at him slowly, "for us to, er, see each other." She noticed her pulse was suddenly racing. Despite the cool cotton fabric of the dress Mrs. H had chosen for her, Bree could feel her face flushing with sudden heat. Beads of sweat gathered at her hairline and the nape of her neck. The fork in her hand twitched a little.

Richard said nothing for a long moment, moving a french fry around the rim of his plate. "Well, that's where I'm going tonight. Angel Cinema, on Alexandra Street. Starts at seven-twenty. Maybe I'll see you there. I'll be sitting somewhere near the middle."

"I think I'm busy tonight," murmured Bree.

"Or do you prefer the front?"

"I-I have to read some scripts," she lied.

"The back, then?"

Bree combed her fingers through her thick red curls. "Uh, look, I have to work—"

"Speaking of which, did you ever get hold of that writer guy, er—what was his name? Roland something."

The Camera-Shy Cupid 65

Bree raised her eyebrows. "Rudolph Gotham. How did—? Oh." She recalled the embarassing incident from the other day. She wiggled her toes. Well, at least Mrs. H had taken pity on her this time and had found some shoes with slightly smaller, less torturous heels.

"Actually, no," she said, glad that the conversation had turned to something less personal. "Turns out Rudolph Gotham gave us an answering service number, and, well, he apparently has no fixed address—just a post office box. But we'll probably meet him soon enough because the script department left a, er, message that BBA wanted to buy his 'Sting Like a Bee' script." She swallowed. "And then they threw the ball into his yard, so to speak."

"What do you mean?"

"They told him they were interested in seeing any other scripts he's written." Bree pursed her lips confidently. "That gets them throwing back the ball pretty quick."

"You think the offer will entice this writer out of hiding, huh?" Richard's expression was oddly unreadable.

"Well, yes. Hopefully. The man certainly has talent," said Bree. "I suspect he might actually be a professional writer—you know, a literary figure."

Richard grinned. "Oh-ho! Now I get it. You're attracted to that type. The serious, bookish, pipe-in-the-mouth kind of guy, huh?"

Bree stared at him, frowning. "Not necessarily." But she said this without conviction. She avoided his gaze, suddenly afraid that he might read too much into her expression. She fixed her attention on the gruesome plate of hard, curled pasta shells in front of her.

"But I'd bet you'd jump at the chance to meet this Rudolph guy, wouldn't you?"

"Well, yes, I suppose—"

"And if he turns out to be some fat, balding slob with bad hygiene?"

Bree pursed her lips. "You know, that old cliché is true; it's not always looks that count. I-I can as easily fall in love with an intellect. Someone who has a fascinating personality—"

"Like me, you mean?" Richard flashed her a boyish grin.

Bree snorted. "I think your mental acuity is beyond me," she retorted sarcastically.

"And my boyish charm overwhelms you, I bet."

"Your self-confidence is staggering. It's obvious you're much too serious and responsible for me," said Bree snidely.

"Hey, I pay my bills on time," said Richard, his indignation showing. He straightened in his chair. "You just have this prejudice against actors, I bet. Well, for your information, Miss Gaston, we actors are not just empty shells. If you'd only get to know me better, you'd find out that inside, I'm quite a fascinating fellow." He winked at her.

"I'm sure you are," she answered. Her patronizing tone hung in the air like a meandering sentence.

Richard sat very still. Then his face suddenly darkened and his features assumed an almost conspiratorial expression. "I think you'd be surprised," he said softly, lifting one eyebrow.

"Cut! And that's a wrap, folks!" cried the man in the ripped jeans.

Bree looked at her watch in astonishment. "That's it?"

"Time flies when you're conversing with fascinating people," said Richard.

The man in the ripped jeans rubbed his eyes, fended off a question from a nearby grip hand, and told everyone to come back on Monday. The noise level in the room suddenly increased and the remainder of his message was drowned out.

The Camera-Shy Cupid 67

Like students let out early on a school day, the excitement about the set was palpable. Everyone spoke at once and moved about—or rather, scurried like a group of mice suddenly set free. Light grips and cameramen hastily shut down their equipment while men and women with clipboards tore off their headsets and dashed toward the exits.

"Monday?" Bree stood up, a mixture of relief and surprise falling into her expression. She could use a few days off.

Richard shoved his hands in his jeans pockets, watching his dinner partner with an inquisitive smile. "Well, since we have some time to kill before the movie, why don't we—"

"Miss Gaston, Mr. Bell," said Bill from Casting, barring their way. He handed them each a card. "Mr. Cromwell and Mrs. Wayne would like to see you both this evening." Bill's hand shot out as he hailed a passing crewman. Before Bree or Richard could say anything he was halfway across the room answering the questions of another extra.

Bree turned the card over in her hand. Susanne Wayne. She recognized the name as being one of the production supervisors for "Sting Like a Bee." The address was a Boise Broadcasting Association casting suite downtown. Her heart performed a small cartwheel when she read the words: EXTRA CASTING AUDITION written in ink on the back of the card.

"Hmmm... seven o'clock," said Richard, gazing up from his card. "I guess we'll have to postpone our plans."

Bree ignored him and gnawed on her lower lip, lost for the moment in her own thoughts. This acting thing was definitely getting out of hand. She had no experience trying out for an acting part, nor, in all this time working in this business, had she ever had the urge or desire to.

Couldn't they see she wasn't an actor? Better to close the door while she still had her hand on the handle—

"Looks like the door has just opened for us," said Richard, distracting Bree from her thoughts. He slipped the card into his jacket pocket. "Today an extra, tomorrow a television star."

Bree followed his gaze to the main set where George Kane was engaged in a heated discussion with Grey Blaine and his costar, Stan Adams. The director's manager, Tom Bronfmann, was playing the role of mediator, attempting to douse the flames that seemed to be rising and getting hotter by the moment. Penny Dowling, accompanied by Gail Sussmann and a glum-looking Charles Cromwell, made their way toward the back exit. The advertising executives who'd attended yesterday's shoot, Bree noticed, were conspicuously absent.

"I think we might still be in the running," Richard mused. "If we can get this bit speaking part on 'Sting Like a Bee'—"

"I wouldn't get my hopes up," said Bree, wincing.

Richard lifted an eyebrow. "Do I detect a note of stage fright? You're not going to fall to pieces on me, are you?"

I'll shatter like crystal, said Bree in silent misery. "Maybe you've forgotten, but I'm not an actor."

A crease appeared between Richard's brows. "Listen, don't get too nervous about it. It's only one acting job. There'll be more."

Bree sighed. "You don't understand. I don't want to get more involved than I have to. I-I was quite content where I was in the reading department."

"Content, were you?" There was a new impatience in his voice. "And here I had you pegged as the wild, adventurous type—not the timid little mouse hiding in her hole, afraid to try anything new."

Timid little mouse? Bree's eyes narrowed slightly.

The Camera-Shy Cupid 69

"Look, just because I don't want to be some glorified, egotistical, show-off *actor*—"

"My, my. You really don't like actors, do you?" said Richard, his lips drawing back slightly over his teeth. "So what was it? A relationship with an actor sour on you? One burnt cookie, and the whole batch is spoiled? Now all actors are jerks, is that it?"

Bree drew back, and blinked in surprise at his sudden hostility. "No, no. Of course not. I just meant—"

"Richie, honey. There you are! I thought we were going to Cantonelli's." Sandy Masterson slipped her hand possessively into his. She flashed Bree a wide, smug smile that did not pretend to be friendly. Her other hand brushed over her glossy hair and then paused to adjust an expensive-looking earring. "Why, hello, Bree," she greeted, as if noticing her for the first time. Her aquamarine eyes swept the length of Bree's long, pale terra-cotta dress, and amusement flitted briefly across her tanned features. "Will you join us?"

Richard's lips twitched. "No, I believe Miss Gaston has other plans."

Bree flushed and clasped her hands together tightly, fighting down the angry retort that hung on the tip of her tongue. But she was frustrated, too, by the anger his remark had roused in her. With a strained smile, she said pertly, "Yes, perhaps another time." And she deliberately turned her back on them, scanning the set for her book bag.

As she gathered her things and headed for the exit, she glimpsed Richard and Sandy Masterson roaring off through the parking lot. The blond woman clung to Richard, her bottle-blond hair flapping against the helmet. Bree watched as she buried her tanned face in the small of his back. Like two pieces of a puzzle fitting snugly and perfectly together, thought Bree. But she wondered at this new feeling, this sudden tightening in her gut.

She shrugged it off, fished some change out of her purse, and went to the far end of the building to call a cab. Lori was there, chatting animatedly on the phone. She greeted Bree with a friendly wave.

"All right, see you in a few minutes," she said into the receiver, and hung up. She smiled at Bree. "Hi. Tough day, huh?" She laughed.

Actually, yes, Bree almost answered. "I could get used to three-day workweeks."

"Oh, it's not always like this. Sometimes Kane pulls us in on the weekends. Once, the film editor ruined an entire week's shoot, and we had to do it all over in two days. Grueling." Lori's eyes widened, remembering. "That was when they first hauled me in as an extra. I was a nervous wreck by the end of the second day. Nearly quit, in fact." She shook her head. "At first I couldn't get used to having those cameras watching me. I had to say a line—real simple, but I kept flubbing it up. Funny thing, though, after a while you start forgetting you're on a television set, being watched by millions of people." She shrugged. "Now it's pretty much routine. I just think to myself *I'm just a waitress serving customers in a restaurant.*"

Bree nodded. *Yes, I'm just a woman having dinner with a man,* she thought. *An attractive, frustrating man who rides a motorcycle and smells of musk and leather—*

"But I guess it's probably different for you. You're a professional," said Lori deferentially.

"Me? Oh, no. I'm not an actor," said Bree quickly.

Lori furrowed her brow. "You could've fooled me. You and Richie have real . . . presence, I'd guess you'd call it. You're not like Paula, Richie's ex-partner. Oh, she's beautiful and everything, legs up to her armpits,

The Camera-Shy Cupid 71

with a great figure. But really, she can't act worth beans! I still can't believe she got a movie deal." Her voice lowered a little. "Of course, sometimes acting talent isn't all you need to get ahead in this business. Paula wasn't exactly a nun."

"Did she and Richard . . . get along?" asked Bree. And she realized, too late, that her voice was markedly edged with jealousy. Bree immediately steeled her expression, hoping Lori wouldn't notice.

But Lori only shrugged. "At one time, yes, I thought they had a thing going. But now, I have a feeling it wasn't mutual."

You mean Richard was in love with Paula, but she didn't return his feelings? said Bree silently. Something suddenly twisted and lurched behind her rib cage. What in the world was wrong with her?

"And I have no idea why he's hanging around Sandy Masterson. Richie used to practically run the other way when she'd come throwing herself at him," said Lori. She turned to Bree. "You know, I thought maybe you two might get together. The way you and Richie look at each other, I almost believe you're in love." Lori swung her bag over her shoulder. "But I guess that's just good acting."

Bree could feel the heat of a blush creeping up from the base of her neck. "Yes," she said, a little too hastily.

Lori regarded her in puzzlement. "You all right? You look a little flushed all of a sudden."

"Indigestion. I ate a bit of that pasta today," Bree lied, forcing out a small laugh.

"I don't know how you extras can eat that stuff with a straight face," said Lori, wrinkling her nose. "I remember this one guy—this was before I was hired on as a waitress. Actually, come to think of it, he was Sandy's ex-dinner companion at the time. Well, they gave him this soup, see? The cook had just dumped the week's leftovers into a big pot and had served it to some of the extras." She chuckled. "Well, this guy ended up choking and spilling it all over Sandy. Oh, boy, was she mad! And the poor guy turned as green as his soup, ran off the set, and never came back." She shook her head. "Kane had a fit."

A white-and-blue van pulled up into the car lot beside them and honked.

"So, what happened to him, this extra?"

Lori turned to the van and waved. Bree glimpsed the dark blue lettering across its flank: SAL'S SOUP EMPORIUM.

"Oh"—Lori smiled wryly—"I married him."

The driver, a man with broad shoulders and a shock of red bristly hair, grinned at them through the front window.

"Hey, you need a ride somewhere?" Lori asked her.

"I was just heading home."

"Great. Hop in. Sal won't mind." Lori took her arm and repeated her address to the man inside.

The three of them sat squished together in the front seat. Sal, whose bulky frame hunched over the steering wheel, smiled genially at her. Lori introduced Bree and he reached across and enveloped her hand in his huge one.

"Bree plays an extra. She's Richard Bell's new partner," said Lori.

Sal's green eyes widened slightly. "Yeah? Richie's a great guy, eh? Real smart, too. I always wondered what he was doing wasting his time in acting. I owe the guy a lot; he helped me start up my business, you know." He batted the fuzzy dice dangling from the front mirror. SOUP, SOUP, SOUP, SOUP; the green-lettered message whirled like a subliminal advertisement.

Lori glanced at Bree. "Richie's a whiz at numbers." She furrowed her brow. "I think he went to the University of Idaho, studied physics, or something."

Bree's eyebrows shot up. The man she knew as Richard

The Camera-Shy Cupid 73

Bell didn't quite fit this academic image they described.

"Three days on the job and Bree's already caught the eye of the producers," Lori said to Sal. She patted Bree's hand. "I heard you and Richie landed a role on 'Sting Like a Bee.' "

Bree groaned under her breath. "Hmmm . . . yes. I—we have an audition tonight, as a matter of fact." She kneaded her hands nervously.

"Audition?" said Sal, impressed. "Not just an extra job, then?"

"Well, I don't think it's—"

"Wow! You and Richie must be excited! A speaking part on 'Sting Like a Bee' could really open doors for you two," said Lori.

Bree uttered a silent moan. Oh, if only she'd closed that door when George Kane had first kidnapped her.

"And I'll bet you anything you and Richie are going to be selected for the Honey-Chew couple. Did you notice Penny Dowling there today, again?" She harrumphed. "And Sandy was so sure she was going to get that part. Today she was bragging in the wardrobe room about her agent having lunch with Penny Dowling, and that she was seriously being considered for the part."

Bree gazed at Lori, confused. The Honey-Chew couple? But Lori didn't seem to notice her quizzical expression.

"I think you and Richie would be perfect for the commercials. You know, like those Canadian herbal tea advertisements? I mean, normally I can't stand commercials, but these ones were so *romantic*."

Sal put his arm around his wife. "Lori's a sucker for romance." He stopped the van at the lights. "Richie's a pretty charming guy—and I guess he's not bad-looking," he added.

Lori pressed her cheek against her husband's arm. "Not as charming or as good-looking as my guy, though."

Sal grinned, pleased. "Yeah, but he's got talent *and* brains."

A lethal combination, thought Bree wanly.

"A perfect combination," said Lori. "Bree, you used to work in the script reading department, right?"

"I still do. This—this extra work is just temporary."

Lori looked at her with a bemused grin. "Oh? But I thought—"

"Left or right?" asked Sal, turning the van onto Hapshire Street.

"Left here on Cranberry Street."

"But if they offer you the Honey-Chew role—"

Bree shook her head. "This extra work is about all I can handle. I'm not really an actor," she said. How many times did she have to repeat this?

"Does Richie know this? I mean, if you two are chosen to be the Honey-Chew couple—"

"They'll have to find someone else," said Bree firmly.

A momentary confusion spread across Lori's face. "I don't understand. Why wouldn't you take it? It would be a wonderful opportunity for both of you, and it would definitely open doors for future roles in television."

Again with the doors. Bree sighed.

"I know the other extras would kill to have this chance," Lori added.

"Well, who knows? Maybe we won't get it," said Bree hopefully.

Lori laughed, squeezing her hand. "Afraid you'll be disappointed, is that it? Listen, Bree, if anyone deserves those roles, it's you and Richie. You're . . . well, you two have a kind of—'spark.' You know what I mean?" She smiled reassuringly. "Just you wait and see. You'll get it, all right."

That's what I'm afraid of, thought Bree, grimacing as Sal nosed the van up into her apartment triplex parking lot.

Chapter Six

"Hi, I'm Penny Dowling." The woman with the short pixie cut shook Bree's hand vigorously. Her face was narrow and sallow-looking, but the brown almond-shaped eyes gleamed with a kind of shrewd energy that made Bree vaguely nervous. "I hope you don't mind me sitting in."

"Oh, no," said Bree, her stomach jumping. "But I should tell you I've never—"

"Miss Gaston, I'm Susanne Wayne. Zachary Chalmers is your agent?"

Bree shook her hand, and let the heavyset woman steer her to the middle of the room. A thick floral scent wafted and puffed about them, seeming to ooze from Susanne Wayne's pores. Bree stifled a sneeze.

"I hear you've come from the script department, is that right?" She didn't wait for Bree's answer. "So I suppose I won't have to explain the concept of our little mystery series, then?" She crinkled her face into a smile. Beneath

The Camera-Shy Cupid

the fleshy folds two blue eyes, like tiny periods, studied her with interest.

Bree fought down an uncomfortable flush.

"Hello, there," said a voice behind her.

She turned around slowly to find herself face-to-face with Richard. Her heart gave a small pattering leap, and she clamped her lips together to compose herself.

"Hey, you *are* nervous," he said, frowning a little.

Hasn't anyone been listening? I'm not an actor! she wailed silently.

Charles Cromwell strolled into the room, his face morose and tense. He spoke to a woman carrying a clipboard and motioned to Susanne Wayne.

"It's just a few lines, Bree. Don't sweat it," said Richard gently. "Just follow my lead. Pretend you're in love with me."

Bree shot him a black look.

"Okay! We ready, then?" Susanne Wayne rubbed her pudgy hands together.

Bree glanced at Richard in a small panic. "Don't—don't we have a script?"

"Yes, yes, of course. Carl?"

The man removed two sheets from his clipboard and handed one to each of them. Bree scanned it quickly, silently thanking her mother for having insisted she take all those speed-reading courses. She glanced over at Richard, who looked up from the sheet confidently. Bree fidgeted and reread the passage at the bottom.

MATTHEW AND CAROLINE EMBRACE, ETC. . . .

What exactly did they mean by "ETC. . . ."? Bree caught Richard's quirk of a smile and gnawed on her lip nervously.

"Everything okay? Perhaps you two would like a moment to prepare?" asked Susanne Wayne.

"I'm ready," said Richard, glancing over at Bree.

Bree nodded, although the slight movement filled her head with a sudden dizziness. With heart pumping hard against her ribs, she took a moment to sweep a cursory glance about the room. The luxurious hotellike atmosphere felt vaguely plastic, unreal, with polished cherrywood end tables and overstuffed upholstered chairs placed about the perimeter. Someone flicked on the overhead light and the room brightened suddenly. Bree's self-consciousness heightened as she realized that she and Richard were being spotlighted.

Susanne Wayne set up the scene, speaking in a low, storytelling voice. "And here's where you come in, Richard."

Richard reached for Bree's hand and uttered his lines perfectly. But Bree could barely hear them over the pumping of her own heart and the blood roaring in her ears.

He squeezed her hand as she hesitated. Richard smiled encouragingly. Bree opened her mouth, but no words came.

"Bree? That's your cue, dear," prompted Susanne.

Bree nodded, bit her lip. "Matthew, I—" She blinked, drew a breath. "Listen, could we start over?"

Charles Cromwell made a small guttural noise and shifted in his chair. Penny Dowling recrossed her legs, watching them with her shrewd eyes.

"Take your time," said Susanne Wayne patiently.

Richard leaned toward her and whispered. "Remember, 'elephant shoes.'"

Bree cocked a frustrated eyebrow and drew herself rigid. "Watermelon," she replied tartly. But in that moment she became aware of the exchange of sudden interested looks between the producers. And Bree found herself relaxing, the tension slowly easing out of her as Richard began again.

They played out the scene, Bree feeling as though Rich-

The Camera-Shy Cupid 79

ard were hypnotizing her with those deep blue eyes. As they approached the end, Bree had the faint sensation of falling, the walls of the hotel suite dissolving around her, the people in the room forgotten. And when Richard wrapped his arms around her, she did not resist. His lips brushed her cheek, then found her mouth. Before Bree realized what he was doing, she was kissing him back.

"Wonderful!" Susanne Wayne clapped. "That's what we want."

Bree broke away, her expression startled. Richard grinned back at her wolfishly, his blue eyes twinkling. Indignation surged through her and two pink spots of anger flamed her cheeks.

"Why, you—"

"Well, what did you think the 'etcetera' meant?"

Susanne put her pudgy hands on their shoulders. "You two have good instincts. Whew! Is it hot in here?" She laughed, her tiny blue eyes disappearing inside the doughy folds of her face. "Right. That's exactly what I want to see on Friday."

"Friday?" Bree inquired. Her stomach muscles tightened.

"Excuse me. Mr. Bell? Miss Gaston?" Penny Dowling approached them. "I think I've made up my mind." The overhead light shone in her shrewd eyes, her excitement evident. She folded her arms across her chest. "How would you two like to be the 'Honey-Chew Couple'?"

Bree felt suddenly nauseated.

A wide grin broke out across Richard's face. "You got yourself a deal, Miss Dowling," he said, shaking her hand vigorously.

"Miss Gaston?"

All eyes turned to her, waiting for her response.

"Cantaloupe," answered Bree, clutching her stomach.

Richard's smile wavered. He gave her a sidelong look. "Uh, she means yes."

Susanne Wayne thumped her on the back, causing Bree's stomach to flip-flop and tighten like a knot.

"Well done!" said the heavyset woman, and Penny Dowling smiled, while Charles Cromwell grunted his approval from his chair. Carl, the man with the clipboard, winked at her.

"Philippe?" said Penny Dowling, turning to the far corner of the room.

Bree observed for the first time the outline of a man seated silent and obscured in the shadow. She watched him rise and stride languidly into the light. His dark eyes devoured hers as his head tilted back slightly in quiet scrutiny.

"Beautiful," he said. His voice belied a heavy accent that was unmistakably French. "Yes, you were right, Penny. *Quelle belle femme.*" He smiled at Bree.

"Bree Gaston, Richard Bell—may I present Philippe Descartes," Penny introduced them. "Philippe is the managing representative of the Honey-Chew ad campaign."

"*Enchanté,* Mademoiselle Gaston." Philippe gently clasped Bree's hand and kissed it, his lips lingering there for a brief moment as his dark eyes flickered up at her.

Bree blushed self-consciously. "Nice to meet you, er, Mr. Descartes."

"Descartes," mused Richard. "Any relation to René?" He extended his hand, his expression tinged with a sudden coolness.

Philippe looked at him, the momentary bemusement in his expression giving way to sudden comprehension as he shook Richard's hand. "Oh, yes. I see now. *'Je pense, donc je suis.'* 'I think, therefore I am.'" He chuckled. "Alas, no, I am no relation to the famous René Descartes.

The Camera-Shy Cupid 81

I am hardly a philosopher—merely a humble businessman."

"Humble, indeed!" harrumphed Susanne Wayne. "Philippe only runs one of the world's largest commercial advertising agencies."

Philippe's lips drew tight, his jaw muscle twitching with suppressed annoyance. "I fear Madame Wayne exaggerates." He turned to address Richard and Bree; his attention, however, was unmistakenly fixed on Bree. "Yes, I definitely approve of Mademoiselle Dowling's choice."

"Good. Then it's settled," said Penny Dowling with a satisfied nod and a quick motion of her hand. Bree could see the thoughts and ideas already churning in her head. "We'll prepare the contracts and send them to you immediately. I'd like to start shooting a week from Monday." She shook Bree's and Richard's hands, an indication that the meeting was over.

"A week from Monday?" stammered Bree.

Charles Cromwell ran his fingers through his thinning blond hair. "I'll have to clear this with George." He sighed.

Philippe Descartes smiled at Bree, adjusting the cuffs of his black serge suit jacket. His dark hair gleamed raven-black in the light, his chiseled features reminding her of those aristocratic marble sculptures she always saw featured in the hallways of the homes in *Dream Homes of America*. He moved elegantly, sleekly, with the poise of a panther moving about his territory. After a moment, Bree realized she was staring at him, and she quickly averted her eyes, embarrassed.

"May I offer you a lift somewhere, Mademoiselle Gaston?" he asked suddenly.

Bree could feel Richard stiffen beside her.

"Philippe, uh, we still have some things to discuss—" began Penny Dowling.

Philippe reluctantly drew his attention away from Bree, his frown denoting his obvious displeasure at having to return to the business at hand. "Well, perhaps sometime we might get together for a drink, Mademoiselle Gaston?"

"Uh, yes. I'd like that," said Bree. She could hear the breathlessness in her answer, and she cursed her own social awkwardness. But this man's sophistication and unwavering confidence made her teeter a little inside, as if she were tipping slightly off balance.

The Frenchman brought her hand to his lips. "May I call for you, then? Shall we say, tomorrow evening?"

"Yes—No!" *Come to my apartment? Oh, no!* She thought about the week's dishes stacked in the sink, her clothes strewn about the living room. When was the last time she'd vacuumed? Dusted? And the horror of her bathroom—

"No?" He gazed at her, confused; Richard watched him, a vague smugness tugging at the corners of his grin.

"I mean, uh, maybe you'd better call me—?"

"Yes, yes. Of course. I shall ring you, first."

"We have that extra job on 'Sting Like a Bee' tomorrow, remember?" said Richard sharply.

"Right," said Susanne Wayne, herding them toward the door. "I'd like you two to come in a little earlier, if you can. Shooting starts at—?" She turned to Charles Cromwell.

"Three," replied Cromwell. "George is going to be royally ticked about this. You know how he gets about sharing extras—"

"Try to be there by two, two-thirty. Right?" She nodded without waiting for their response. "Right! Well, now that's settled—"

"Thank you for coming, Bree, Richard. I look forward to working with you both." Penny Dowling opened the door.

Bree glanced back as the door shut behind them. She shook her head. What had just happened in there? She found that she was trembling a little, perspiration suddenly gathering under her arms.

"*'Enchanté, Mademoiselle Gaston,'*" Richard mimicked with a sneer. "Can you believe that guy? Who does he think he is? Hercules Poirot?"

"Hercules Poirot is Belgian," said Bree, gnawing on her lip. She groaned aloud. "I can't believe I said yes."

"Me neither. I didn't think you'd fall for that kind of fake charm. Although he did lay it on pretty thick, I thought."

"What—? Oh, no. I mean that Honey-Chew couple thing. I never dreamed we'd actually—" She sighed. "I can't act. Couldn't they see that?"

Richard gazed at her, his blue eyes scanning her face. He pressed the elevator button. "I think tonight you just proved yourself wrong, Bree. You ever think that maybe you *are* an actress? I don't know why you just don't admit it—"

The elevator doors opened. Bree hesitated, then stepped inside. Richard followed silently. They stood, waiting.

"I suppose one of us should press a button," said Bree after a moment.

Richard's brows twitched. He reached over and thumbed the bottom button. The elevator gave a brief shudder and lurched into motion. They descended for two seconds, then suddenly jerked to a stop. The doors in front of them remained closed.

"What happened?"

"I don't know," said Richard. He tried the lobby button again. The elevator didn't move.

"Wha—?"

The lights went out.

"Uh-oh. Just a second."

Beside her, Bree heard Richard searching through his leather jacket pocket. "Ah, here." He struck a match and held it up to her face. "My, how beautiful you look by firelight, Mademoiselle Gaston," he said in a thick French accent.

Bree glowered at him impatiently. "Maybe you'd better pull the emergency cord."

"Do I detect a note of nervousness in your voice, Mademoiselle Gaston? Perhaps that kiss awakened in you some animal instinct—"

"Listen, Sherlock, the only instinct that kiss roused in me was to stay as far away from you as possible."

"Oh? I think the lady doth protest too much. Ow!" Richard threw down the match, blowing on his fingers. The flame promptly winked out and they were in darkness again.

"Wonderful. Well? Light another match."

Richard uttered a sheepish gurgle from his throat. "Hmmm . . . I do believe that was my one and only match. You wouldn't happen to—"

"Oh, this is just great." Bree reached over blindly toward the button panel just as the elevator hummed back to life. The sudden jerking motion made her stumble and pitch forward. She fell against him and Richard caught her, holding her close in the dark. His chin brushed her cheek, and she drank in the sweet, manly smell of him. The elevator began to descend again, and an instant later the lights flicked on.

"Well, hello there," he murmured into her hair. His arms tightened around her shoulders.

The doors slid open and two elderly men in suits stood

The Camera-Shy Cupid

staring at them. Flushing, Bree pushed her way out of the embrace and stalked out.

Richard followed her through the corridor, waved to the receptionist at the desk, and hurried to catch up with Bree at the revolving exit.

"Heh, heh, baby, you need a ride home?" he asked, putting on one of his most lecherous grins.

"I'll take a cab," she said tartly.

Richard took her arm. "Aw, come on. I promise I'll be a good boy."

She let him lead her to his motorcycle parked in the back lot, too weary now to argue. "I live on—"

"Cranberry Street. Yes, I know," he said, donning his helmet. He took in her inquisitive look. "I just happened to see it on the casting sheet," he said, his grin widening. He shook his head. "Nah, actually, I ran into Sal earlier today. He and Lori seem to think—" He abruptly cut himself off, his brows suddenly drawing together pensively. He grimaced slightly and nodded to the helmet. "Better put that on."

Bree climbed onto the back of the bike, and with but a moment's hesitation, folded her arms gently about his waist. But as they roared out onto the street, she clutched at him tightly. They sped northward toward Cranberry Street, and Bree's thoughts and concerns fled with the increasing speed of the motorcycle. She bent her head back, feeling the cool wind whip at her hot, flushed face. And for the first time that day, she began to relax and enjoy herself.

When Richard halted in front of her apartment triplex, Bree almost wished that they could keep riding. And, as if reading her thoughts, Richard took the helmet from her and gave her an understanding smile.

"Nothing like a good bike ride to clear the head. Ol' Maggie here helps keep me sane." He patted the seat affectionately. "Whenever I get writer's—" He bit his lip. "Whenever I get tense, or my nerves are shot, I just hop on Ol' Maggie here and ride. Never fails to put things into perspective."

Bree nodded, brushing her hair away from her eyes. "I think I know what you mean." She felt a sudden shyness creep into her smile as he took a step closer. His eyes lingered over her face, resting for a moment on her lips.

"Well, I guess I'll see you tomorrow." He turned away from her, and straddled his motorcycle. And without looking back, he roared away.

Bree watched him, and closed her eyes. Her fingertips went instinctively to her lips.

"Nice fellow," murmured a gruff voice behind her. Bree jumped back in alarm. A scruffy-looking man emerged from the shadow. He held out a paper bag molded into the shape of a bottle. Bree let out a relieved breath.

"Hello, Mr. Braxton. How are you tonight?" greeted Bree.

Old Mr. Braxton lived in the basement, but most days he just wandered about the building with the same empty whiskey bottle. He was a fixture here, and though some of the tenants complained about his vagrant behavior, Bree tended to view the old man's presence more as a kind of friendly gargoyle watching over the place. She gazed at his sallow skin, noting the sunken cheekbones and sad gray eyes.

"Hey, I've got some leftover pizza in the fridge. You hungry, Mr. Braxton?"

The old man flashed her a gummy smile and winked with the side of his bony face. "Naw, I had my fill tonight, sweetie, thank you." He patted his stomach. "Your young man there, he came by earlier tonight—just after you left."

"He did?"

"I told him you'd gone out. He left, then came back. Brought me a hot turkey sandwich." He smacked his lips. "Best sandwich I ever et, it was." He nodded to himself. "Yep, a nice young fellow, he is."

Bree stared at Mr. Braxton. "Uh, yes. That was nice of him," she said, furrowing her brow.

"Said I reminded him of his uncle back in..." Mr. Braxton scratched his head. "I can't recall now where he said he was from. Virginia? Indiana, maybe it was..." His voice trailed incoherently, and Bree watched as the old man's eyes glazed over, drifting back into his foggy world.

She bade him good night and left him there on the front steps, steeped in his own private thoughts. As Bree climbed the steps up to her apartment, her head buzzed with new thoughts and questions of her own.

It took her a moment to finally admit to herself that she might very well have misjudged Richard Bell. She'd automatically slotted him in with all those other actors she'd dated: egotistic, selfish, altogether too self-involved. She'd pegged him as a man who didn't have a serious bone in his body: the immature, insensitive type. Could she have been wrong?

The phone rang, jarring her out of her reverie. She leaped for it.

"Hello?"

"So, you never did tell me. What did you think of that kiss?"

"What?" Bree blinked, then suddenly recognized Richard's voice.

"I mean, on a scale of one to ten—it was right up there, wouldn't you say? Come on, you can tell me."

Bree stared at the receiver in disbelief.

"Hello? Bree? You still there?"

Bree shook her head.

"Maybe we should practice a little more. You know, to get it right—"

"Elephant shoes," she said loudly.

A beat passed between them.

"Yeah," he said huskily. "Me, too. See you tomorrow," and he hung up.

Bree slammed down the receiver. In her mind's eye she could see that smug grin of his, his blue eyes twinkling with self-amusement. Oh, she'd pegged him all right.

She looked at her watch: 8:52 P.M. With a long, resigned sigh she began dialing Zachary's number.

Chapter Seven

Zachary collected the papers on the coffee table and filed them in his briefcase. "Bree, I don't know why you're tying yourself up in knots over this. Anyone would think this was the worst thing that ever happened to you."

"Zachary, how'd I get myself into this?" she moaned, cradling her head in her hands. "You're sure I'm okay signing these?"

"Your soul's not in danger, if that's what you mean," said Zachary, chuckling. "The contract's pretty standard. They're paying for everything: the flight, the accommodations—"

"Where is this town, Grable, anyway? I've never heard of it."

"It's just south of British Columbia."

"British Columbia, Canada?"

"Think of it as a vacation. Maybe you can go visit your folks while you're there." He glanced at his watch. "It's nearly four. I'd better get you over to the set."

"My parents live on the other side of the country. You know how big Canada is?"

Zachary squinted one eye. "Let's see . . . three million, eight hundred and forty—no, fifty-one—thousand, eight hundred and nine square miles—give or take a mile."

Bree stood up with a disgusted look on her face.

"Oh, by the way, I was talking to Susanne Wayne about the script you gave me. She's as anxious to talk to this Rudolph Gotham as you are. And it seems you and Richard really impressed her last night, because she's considering you two for the starring roles."

"No, no way. Absolutely not." Bree shook her head vehemently. "After this Honey-Chew thing, I'm retiring from the acting business."

Zachary let out a puzzled breath, then shrugged his shoulders in defeat. "And here I thought I was finally getting somewhere in this agenting business."

"I'm sorry, Zachary," said Bree. "But you did know I was going back to my old job at the script reading department."

"I was hoping you'd change your mind—speaking of which, did I tell you we received another script from Rudolph Gotham?"

"Oh? Another 'Sting Like a Bee' script?" she asked, her interest suddenly piqued.

Zachary shook his head. "Uh-uh. This time he wrote an episode for "The Camera-Shy Cupid." And it's really funny. I heard Grey Blaine isn't too keen about it, though—probably because he didn't cowrite it. But Cromwell and Gail Sussmann have already bought the script."

"Really? So, does this mean we're finally going to meet this Rudolph Gotham?" said Bree excitedly. "I wonder what he's like."

"Wonder all you like. Mr. Gotham has refused to come out of hiding."

The Camera-Shy Cupid

Bree looked disappointed. "How strange. You'd think—" "We'd better get a move on. I have to drop these contracts off and I still have some unfinished work at the office." He shrugged on his jacket. "By the way, I got a call from Philippe Descartes this morning. He asked me a lot of questions about you."

Bree paused in her step, her gray eyes snapping to attention. "Really? What kind of questions?"

"Actually, they were pretty personal," said Zachary, frowning reflectively. He glimpsed her apprehensive expression and gave her a reassuring smile. "Quit worrying. I didn't tell him anything unsavory about you. He mostly wanted to know if you were unattached, if you were seeing anybody at the moment. Stuff like that."

"And what'd you tell him? No, never mind—" She scrunched up her eyes and waved her hand at him. "I don't want to know." She scratched her head. "Isn't that, uh, rather unusual? Calling up someone's agent to ask personal questions like that?"

Zachary grinned and winked at her. "Seems he's not the only one making 'unusual inquiries' these days."

What's that supposed to mean? she was about to ask. Who else would be asking personal questions about her? But Zachary was already opening her apartment door and shooing her out.

Susanne Wayne apologized to Bree and Richard, explaining that they were running behind schedule due to an unforeseen development involving one irritable costar and a cat. The director, a young man with frizzy hair and thick spectacles, finally emerged from the back dressing room with one of the stars of "Sting Like a Bee." The woman sneezed behind him, cursed loudly, and glared about her murderously. The cat and its trainer were hastily ushered off the set.

Bree and Richard leaned against the hotel bar, waiting. They'd been there for over an hour now.

"This is insane," mumbled Bree.

"At least they could serve real drinks," said Richard, sipping his mock ginger ale glumly. He looked at Bree with an approving lazy sweep of his eyes. "Maybe we should use this time to practice that kiss for tomorrow."

Bree adjusted the strapless gold lamé dress self-consciously. At her request, Mrs. H had pinned it in the back to make the slope of the front a little less revealing. But still, Bree felt uncomfortably underdressed.

"Why hide such a pretty figure?" Mrs. H had tutted. "You're so young and pretty. And you and Richard make such an attractive couple. Now if I were in your shoes—"

Bree shifted her weight, trying to alleviate the pressure of the tiny pointed toes of her gold heels. Out of the corner of her eye she snuck a peek at her partner, whose gaze was momentarily distracted by the bartender extra rearranging for the umpteenth time the glasses at the back of the bar. With hand in his trouser pocket and elbow propped up on the bar counter, Richard appeared wholly at ease. The tuxedo lent his trim figure an elegance and sophistication that rather disappointed Bree. Indeed, she wanted him to feel as uncomfortable and awkward as she—to burst that bubble of self-confidence that seemed to surround him like an impenetrable force field. Nothing appeared to make a dent. How could anyone be that secure about themselves? she wondered warily.

And too, she was conscious of how attractive he was, standing beside her, rousing in her feelings that warmed her cheeks and made her heart beat a little fiercer and faster. Richard caught her stare and Bree quickly looked away, feigning boredom.

"That Tracy and Hepburn double feature is playing

The Camera-Shy Cupid 93

again tonight," he whispered in her ear. "Starts at seven-twenty."

"Well, have fun," said Bree.

"I guess you don't like those old films."

"I didn't say that."

"Too romantic for you, I suppose."

"I didn't say that, either."

Richard compressed his lips, tilting his head slightly to one side. "You have plans tonight, then."

"I didn't say—"

"Yes, yes. Okay, I get the idea. You'd like to go to the movies, but not with me. All right. You don't have to hit me over the head with that proverbial baseball bat."

They were silent for a few minutes. Bree found herself wishing he would say something. Finally, she spoke, surprised by her own words:

"Well, I might show up."

Richard's lips curved into a grin that quivered slightly as he sought to control it. "Hmmm . . . well. There just might be an empty seat next to me in the theater: tonight, seven-twenty, Angel Cinema on Alexandra Street."

Bree was about to respond—to inform him that this wasn't, in fact, an *official* date—when the frizzy-haired director clapped his hands and announced that shooting was about to begin. Everyone scrambled to their positions. Richard locked his arm around Bree's waist and tried to lead her to the other side of the room, but Bree slapped away his hand.

A walk-on, walk-off part, Bree found out, was exactly what it sounded like. The problem was her heels and the slippery parquet floor. As they strolled toward the exit, with Richard's hand firmly on her back, Bree's foot slipped from under her and she fell clumsily into his arms. It would have been a negligible, barely detectable slip, except that Bree's flailing arm struck the back of another extra actor's head and the man slumped forward, knocking over his water glass, which in turn rolled and hit the base of the candelabra. The candelabra teetered and fell, and the cheap lacy tablecloth caught fire. The extras swiftly doused the flames with water as the frizzy-haired director balled his fists in frustration and yelled: *"Cut!"*

Bree felt as though it were she who had been set on fire. Mortified, she apologized to the scrabbling crewmen, assuring the director, who gazed at her with barely suppressed impatience, that she was unhurt. Richard watched the entire scene with a nonchalant expression, though he was unable to veil the twinkle of amusement in his eyes.

"You'd better leave out 'walking' on your résumé," he whispered teasingly.

"It's these darn shoes," grumbled Bree.

The second take went a little more smoothly. Later, however, when Bree would watch this episode on television, her embarrassment would be at its peak, for her clumsily maneuvered strides were reminiscent of an elderly lady with very bad hips. And with these careful, staccatolike steps, it seemed to Bree to take them a lifetime to get from one end of the room to the other. But as soon as they exited the scene, Bree snatched off the heels, cursing under her breath.

Richard whistled "Farewell, Amanda" between his teeth. He pulled down the brim of an invisible hat and said in a singsong voice: "Seven-twenty," and strolled off cheerfully with hands in his pockets.

Bree took a long deep breath and massaged the spot of pain that had suddenly appeared above her right eye.

"Mademoiselle Gaston," said a voice behind her.

She turned around in time to see Philippe Descartes stepping out from one of the side rooms. A woman trailed

The Camera-Shy Cupid   95

him, smoothing out her tight skirt, and fixing her hair. Bree recognized Sandy Masterson immediately.

"Miss Bree Gaston, this is Miss Sandy—"

"We know each other," interrupted Sandy. She smiled a sickly sweet smile, running her tongue over her pink-frosted mouth.

"Ah, good," said Philippe. But he shifted his gaze to Sandy, then back to Bree, his expression uncertain. Indeed, the tension in the corridor had grown palpable.

"Sandy! We're on!" Sandy's blond ponytailed partner beckoned her from the door of the set.

Sandy leveled her gaze on Bree. Her eyes, Bree remarked curiously, were now a violet blue, the exact color of Sandy's dress.

"Congratulations on winning the Honey-Chew role," she said with an insincere smile. She glanced at Philippe Descartes. "I guess I'll be seeing you in Grable." And she swiveled off, hips swaying alluringly, slinking toward the set entrance where her partner fussed with his hair and breathed into his hands, checking his breath.

The Frenchman lifted his brows. "She's perfect for the, er, temptress—the female villain, as you would call her. Don't you think?"

Bree didn't know what in the world he was talking about, but she nodded in agreement. What kind of commercial were they making, anyway?

"Are you free for dinner this evening, Bree?" Philippe asked, smiling. "Oh, may I call you Bree?"

"Sure. Yes, uh, Mr. Descartes—"

"Philippe, please. We will be working together, after all. It is much easier to communicate on a first-name basis, don't you think?"

Bree returned his smile. The man before her had exchanged his black serge suit of last night for a designer denim shirt and jeans. With his *GQ* poise and classic features, he held a startling likeness to one of those male models posing for a magazine advertisement.

He gazed quizzically down at her high heels clenched in her hands. "Your shoes—they are broken?" He took a step forward and studied them.

"Uh, no. I'm-I'm just not used to walking in these—" *Torture devices,* she almost said.

"I shall pick you up at seven, then?"

"Seven?"

"This is too late? Would you prefer I pick you up at six? Six-thirty? Americans like to eat early. Perhaps five?"

"N-no. Seven is fine. It's just—" Bree was remembering the chaotic state of her apartment before she left this afternoon. "How—how about I meet you?"

Philippe gazed at her. Uncomprehension flitted momentarily across his handsome, chiseled European face. But he only shrugged, his dark eyes alight with sudden new curiosity. "Certainly. If that is your wish. Er, let us say . . . the Silver Chalice, for seven o'clock, yes?"

The Silver Chalice? Even the President of the United States had to make a reservation for that place. Bree swallowed back the sudden dryness that rose up in her throat. "The Silver Chalice. Yes, all right," she said hoarsely.

"Good. I look forward to seeing you, Bree," he said, pleased.

It was not until she stumbled back into the wardrobe room that Bree remembered her date with Richard.

"I'm sorry. We're not allowed to give out personal information," said the woman on the other end.

"But this is important—"

"I'm sorry. That's company policy."

Bree hung up and flipped open the phone book. She groaned when she saw the two-page listing of Bells. A

The Camera-Shy Cupid 97

third of the names included the initial 'R'; astonishingly enough, none of them 'Richard.' Bree began dialing.

"Hello, may I speak to Richard Bell?"

"Sorry, no one here by that name."

"Uh, hi. Is there a Richard Bell there?"

"No. You must have the wrong number."

"Hello. I'm looking for Richard Bell?"

"Richard? You sure you don't mean Robert Bell?"

"Good evening. I was wondering if I might speak to Richard?"

"Who? Who izz dis speakeeng? I no understand. No spik inglish good, eh? Who izz..."

Bree hung up and read the last R. Bell listed in the phone book. She punched in the numbers.

"Richard? Yes, just a moment," said a woman. Bree could hear her hollering in the background.

Gee, thought Bree, *does he live with his parents?*

A small, tinny voice answered. "Hello?"

"Richard? Uh, it's Bree."

"Bree? Bree who?" And then, without muffling the receiver, he shouted: "Mom! Do I know a Bree?"

And Bree suddenly realized she was speaking to a child. "Oh, I'm sorry. I think I have the wrong Richard Bell." She hung up with a wince. She stared at the phone and shook her head in frustration. Leave it to Richard to have an unlisted number.

She slumped back against the couch, thinking. Well, it wasn't really a date. Not really. She'd told Richard she *might* show up at the theater. It wasn't as if their plans had been definite or anything. Surely Richard would understand if she didn't show up. After all, it wasn't every day someone like her got a chance to dine at the Silver Chalice—and certainly not with a man like Philippe Descartes. *Yes, Richard will understand,* she told herself.

Bree plodded into her bedroom and stared at the cream

dress hanging on her closet door. Mrs. H had agreed to loan it to her for the night. She touched the delicate serge cotton, letting it slip between her fingers admiringly. Pretty, but not too garish. Classy, elegant; appropriate for an evening at the Silver Chalice. The shoes Mrs. H had selected were a slightly darker color of cream, with delicate but sensible-enough heels. Bree slipped them on and strode about her apartment. Yes, they would do fine.

By six-thirty-five she was dressed and ready. Her heart thumped excitedly in her chest, and low in her abdomen butterflies began to flutter. But, too, there was a persistent nagging that tugged at the back of her mind, and as she gazed at her reflection she saw that her lips were twitching a little.

"Don't be silly, Bree. You can go to the movies anytime." She gave herself a disapproving look and tossed back her head, her red curls cascading prettily about her shoulders. "Spencer Tracy and Katharine Hepburn will just have to wait." She gathered up her purse and strode deliberately out the door, pausing to take a deep breath. Where was this anxiety coming from?

Old Mr. Braxton waved to her, grinning. "Off to see your young man?"

Bree smiled and waved back as she climbed into the waiting taxi.

"Where to, miss?"

"Uh, the Silver Chalice, please."

The driver gave a low whistle and glanced back at her in the rearview mirror. After a moment, he said, "Forgive me for saying this, miss, but have I seen you before? You're not, by chance, in the movies?"

Bree snorted. "Me? No, I'm not in the movies." *I'm on television,* she jeered silently. Could the driver have recognized her from "The Camera-Shy Cupid"? she won-

The Camera-Shy Cupid 99

dered. But no, that was impossible; those episodes hadn't even aired yet.

"You an actor on television, then?" the driver asked after a beat.

"Television? Well, I—" Bree hesitated. "No," she lied. And really, it wasn't much of a lie; after all, she wasn't *really* an actor.

The taxi driver uttered a disappointed "oh," and lapsed into silence.

They drove up to the building whose romantic castle-like turrets shimmered a silvery chrome. Bree watched a middle-aged couple being escorted from their Mercedes sedan across the carpeted route through to the portal entrance. Her lemon-yellow cab was highly visible here, a naked light bulb in a sea of antique brass lanterns. Bree gazed down at her dress nervously, checking her loose curls in her reflection in the cab window.

A sudden thought strayed into her mind, and she hesitated. For several minutes she sat there in the backseat of the taxi trying to exorcise this thought, trying to convince herself to get out of the cab and go meet Philippe Descartes.

"Miss? We're here, miss." The driver was gazing at himself in the flap mirror, licking his stubby fingers and wetting down his stubborn cowlick. "That'll be—"

"Listen, will you wait here for a second?" *What are you doing, Bree?* But before she could answer herself, she had stepped out of the cab and was sidling up to one of the escorts garbed formally in black tails and top hat.

"Good evening, Madame." The young escort bowed.

"Good evening," she said nervously. "Uh, could you help me? I'm, uh, supposed to meet someone here. His name is Philippe Descartes."

Recognition immediately lit in the escort's eyes. "Yes.

Monsieur Descartes has already arrived. He is waiting for you in the bar, Miss Gaston. Shall I escort you?"

Bree cringed at the reverential tone with which he spoke her name. She smiled her best rueful smile (which was never successful for her in the past). "Could you possibly do something for me? Could you tell Mr. Descartes that I am sorry, but that something, uh, came up, and that I am unable to dine with him this evening?"

The escort did not bat an eye, the gravity of his expression deepening only slightly. But there was no inquiry or curiosity in his answer. "Yes, of course, Miss Gaston."

Bree thanked him and returned to the taxi.

"Miss?" The cab driver looked slightly startled as she dove into the back of the taxi and began rummaging through her handbag.

Bree found her watch and looked at it: 6:29 P.M. That couldn't be the right time. She held the watch to her ear and shook it anxiously. "What time is it?"

"Three minutes after seven, Miss."

"Take me to the Angel Cinema," she said, leaning back against the seat with a sigh. "And you'd better step on it."

She paid the driver as he screeched to a halt before the theater. With the skirt of her dress bunched up in her hand, she bounded up the steps of the old, rambling building.

"Has it already started?" she asked the ticket girl breathlessly.

The girl eyed Bree's elegant vestiture with raised brows. "*Woman of the Year* started two minutes ago."

Bree bought a ticket and gestured to the usher, who did a double take as he led her with his flashlight into the darkened theater. Bree was too busy fighting with her rational mind to feel self-conscious. She looked up at the

The Camera-Shy Cupid 101

screen; she couldn't believe she'd given up an evening at the Silver Chalice—for this.

She picked him out immediately. The back of his head seemed all too familiar, and upon spying him, a new shyness gripped her. Richard sat slumped down in his seat, eating from a jumbo-size popcorn. Bree moved down the row and took the seat next to him. Richard glanced over at her expressionlessly.

"You're late," he mumbled.

"I'm here, aren't I?" she snapped back. Irritation began to mount in her chest, and she bit her lip. If he started in on her for being late—

"Yes, you are here," he said with a grin. His eyes took on a warm glow as he gazed at her. "Popcorn?"

"Thanks." Bree reached into the box sighing inwardly. Right about now at the Silver Chalice they would be serving appetizers: calamari, maybe? Or those little stuffed mushrooms she liked so much. Mmm . . . moussaka. Bree visualized a tray laden with bruschetta and fried zucchini.

Richard's hand grazed hers, the touch drawing Bree out of her thoughts. He gave her fingers a light squeeze.

"Thanks for coming," he whispered.

Bree fought back her own grin, but found that she could not. Her heart soared with the romantic theme music of the opening of *Woman of the Year*, and an unfamiliar contentment filled her belly as she sighed back into the seat happily. For the next four hours or so she allowed the magic of the movies to enfold her and sweep her away.

Chapter Eight

Richard blinked as they emerged from the darkened theater. He looked over at Bree, and wonderment crossed his face. But it was quickly overtaken by a teasing grin that had a covetous look about it. He cocked an approving eyebrow at Bree. "So this is what you wear to the movies, eh? Trying to impress me?"

Bree's smile flattened. "Don't flatter yourself."

"Perhaps you were expecting me to take you to the Silver Chalice?"

She knew it was merely a facetious remark, only light teasing, but she blushed anyway, and she was angry at herself for reacting so. Were her thoughts so transparent? For indeed, not a moment ago, Bree had been thinking about what it would be like to dine at the Silver Chalice.

But her mood was now infused with that dreamy romantic feeling she'd often get just after coming out of the movies. Bree smiled wistfully to herself, pretending for a moment that she was Katharine Hepburn: Woman of the Year, Adam's "rib"—

"Women always have to make things so complicated," said Richard, as if musing to himself. "Why can't they just come right out and say what they want? It's like they're toying with us, making us their pawns." He frowned in irritation. "But then, most women don't know what they want, do they?"

Bree glanced about the drifting theater crowd, and bunched up her lips. There was something almost certainly insulting, she thought, in his remark. "Well, it's late. I'd better be heading home," she said curtly. "I'll call a taxi."

Richard stared at her. "See? That's exactly my point."

"Excuse me?"

"You don't want to go home."

"I don't?"

Richard shook his head. "No. You don't want to call a taxi, either."

Bree rolled her eyes, a sigh of exasperation escaping her lips. "So when I say I want to call a cab and go home, this means that I actually want to stay here with you."

Richard's blue eyes sparkled, the laughter in them deepening their color. His lips twisted in obvious enjoyment of the moment. "Okay," he said.

Bree frowned. "Okay, what?"

"Okay, I'll take you out for pizza."

"But I just said—"

Richard grabbed her arm. "Trust me." He slipped his hand into hers and entwined her fingers in his. He pulled her toward the exit. "You'll love this place."

"Wait here." Richard kicked the stand and leaped off the bike. "This'll only take a minute."

Bree gazed up at the flashing orange and red lights that lit up the word: PEEZA! A warm, spicy aroma drifted out to where she stood in the tiny parking lot, and she hugged herself, enjoying the warm night air. Behind the windows with their red-and-white checked curtains she spotted Richard. He and an older man with long gray sideburns were engaged in an animated conversation. The older man waved his hands in the air, as if to emphasize a point, and Richard suddenly threw back his head and laughed.

Bree narrowed her eyes suspiciously. Were they talking about her? She smoothed the folds of her cream dress self-consciously, and noticed with horror the smudge of grease on the skirt hem. Mrs. H was going to kill her! Bree rubbed at it frantically.

Oh, why had she chosen to go to the theater? She must be deranged to have chosen pizza over lobster bisque . . . hmmm, or veal Bourgignon. Her mouth watered. Richard waved to her behind a fog of steam. She waved back uncertainly.

She turned around and shook her head. A yellow cab whooshed by, and Bree almost hailed it. Suddenly she felt a little uneasy about having put herself in the hands of this unpredictable man—this *actor*.

"Okay!" Richard burst out of the PEEZA! place bearing a long rectangular package. "We're all set!" He twirled it around on his hand like a waiter's tray, tossed it in the air, caught it, and deftly slid it sideways into the bike satchel.

Bree bit her lip, hesitating. "Look, if you think I'm going back to your place—"

"Nope. Sorry to disappoint you," said Richard straddling the seat. "As much as I'd love to show you my etchings, well, frankly, I don't think I know you quite well enough. And truthfully? I'm not sure I can trust you."

The Camera-Shy Cupid 105

"*Me?* Not trust *me?*" Bree shook her head, flabbergasted.

"Hop on. The pizza's getting cold already, and here I had it specially made." He gestured behind him and revved the bike.

Bree passed a hand over her red curls and scratched the back of her head. But she put on the helmet and climbed onto the seat behind him, careful to gather up the skirt of her dress. With a burst of speed, Richard took them through the streets, passing several cars along their route. Bree's arms clung about Richard's waist, the wind stinging her face and eyes.

Her hair flew across her eyes, obscuring her vision, and she pressed her face into his back. She glanced up just as they veered off the main road and rode into a man-size culvert.

"Where are we going?" she shouted.

They bumped out of the tunnel and Bree gasped as the motorcycle swerved sharply to the left. But Richard was in control, and they were soon traveling an unpaved road that began to wind toward the foothills. Bree surveyed the unfamiliar terrain and stiffened in her seat. Richard, sensing her sudden nervousness, glanced back to smile at her reassuringly.

A single headlight appeared a distance ahead. Bree saw that it was another motorcycle. The driver flashed his lights as he passed. Richard waved at the bike.

"Who was that?" asked Bree. But she didn't expect an answer, suspecting that the greeting was part of a motorcyle rider's etiquette.

Now flanking the road were juniper trees and tall spruces. The growth of trees grew more congested as they continued up the sloping road. And just as Bree was feeling a touch of claustrophobia, hemmed in by all these trees, the terrain suddenly opened up into a wide, flat clearing. And Bree felt as though the sky, too, had opened up, sprawling over them like a vast canopy of tiny winking lights.

She also noticed, as Richard stopped and cut the bike's engine, that they were alone.

"What is this place?" She climbed off the seat, surprised by the calm in her voice. She shook out her hair as she pulled off the helmet, and gazed about her in wonder.

They appeared to be standing on some leveled precipice. Straight ahead, to their left, and behind them, old knotted pines and juniper trees rose up like a protective fence. To their right the gravel road ribboned northeast and out of sight. The place was deserted. Only the empyrean of stars watched them from above. Suddenly, that old clichéd name, "Inspiration Point," came to Bree's mind. She surveyed the area again, almost expecting to see teenage couples lurking about, kissing in their parents' cars. She chuckled to herself.

Richard tucked a blanket under one arm, balancing the pizza in the other. He flicked on a small light at the side of his bike. With his face drenched in shadows, he looked over at Bree. His lips played into a sober, uncertain smile.

"I come here sometimes when I have writ—I mean, it's a great place to clear your head. You know, just to sit and think."

Bree nodded. "Yes, I can see that. It-it's very ... peaceful," she said, for lack of a better word.

Richard spread out the blanket and produced from the folds a bottle of Coke.

"It's the 'real thing,' " he said, grinning. "I hope you like anchovies."

Bree wrinkled her nose.

Richard laughed. "Aha! You don't like them, either.

Something we both have in common. See? We're not so different."

No, thought Bree, relaxing. *We're not so different.*

They ate the pizza, enjoying the thin crisp crust and spicy sauce, gradually finding themselves falling into an easy conversation.

Perhaps it was this place, Bree mused idly, that had loosened her tongue. Here there were no cameras following their movements, or lights beaming down on them, no silly people with clipboards running around. For indeed, she was surprised at the way she was chatting so openly and effortlessly with this man who lay back on his side, his head propped up lazily by his hand. And Richard, in turn, told her about himself, his usual aloof, off-the-cuff manner slipping away into an uncharacteristic quiet pensiveness.

Bree learned that Richard had worked at several jobs before landing his extra part on "The Camera-Shy Cupid."

"For a while I walked dogs for a living. I'd do this twice a day—eleven dogs."

"Eleven dogs? You mean, all at the same time?"

Richard stroked his chin thoughtfully and grimaced. "I didn't know much about dogs back then. I thought, hey, they're all dogs, right? It'd be like walking one big family. They'd sniff each other's noses and get to know one another. Yeah, they'll all be friends in no time." Richard groaned. "Little did I know."

"So, what happened?"

"The dachshund practically crippled the German shepherd, and the boxer and Mrs. Aberfoyle's toy poodle . . . well, they got a little romantic, if you know what I mean."

Bree laughed.

"I heard they ran off together and are now living somewhere in L.A.," said Richard, taking a bite of his pizza. "They've probably landed a role in some Disney movie by now." He sat up. "Anyway, I quit that job and went to work in a microbiology lab."

"Microbiology?"

Richard made a face as memories began to surface. "Performing lab experiments on viruses is not the most exciting thing in the world, let me tell you." He shook his head. "And then I taught physics at a high school in Indiana for two years." And he went on to describe some of his teaching adventures, with Bree listening, her eyes widening, riveted.

"Hmmm... my life seems so dull compared to yours," she said after Richard prompted her. "I've only had two jobs in my lifetime—"

"A librarian, right?"

Bree grimaced, suddenly thankful that her abashed flush was hidden by the night's shadows. "Am I really that transparent? Yes, I was a research librarian for a while. And then I met Zachary, who helped get me this script-reading job at BBA."

Richard sat up, staring at her. "You really enjoy reading those television scripts?"

"I love it. Oh, it's true, some of the submissions are just awful. But then occasionally you come across some real gems—"

"Like that script I saw the other day."

"Rudolph Gotham's script. Yes, precisely," said Bree enthusiastically. "I think this is a writer to watch. If I'm right, he's going to be big in the television business."

"Yeah? He might also be a flash-in-the-pan, a nobody who just happened to write one good script."

Bree shook her head. "Don't think Zachary and I haven't thought about that. But it looks as though our concerns were unjustified. Zachary told me Rudolph

The Camera-Shy Cupid 109

Gotham sent them another script, this time for 'The Camera-Shy Cupid.' "

"And they're buying it?"

She looked at him hesitantly. "I'm not so sure I should be discussing this with you."

Richard shrugged. He watched her for a moment. The moonlight danced in his eyes, and his teeth gleamed as he leaned toward her. "You just get so excited when you talk about your work; your whole face takes on this... glow." He tilted his head to the side. "I'm almost a little jealous of this Rudolph Gotham guy. Writers, they interest you, don't they?"

"I suppose," said Bree, feeling her face grow hot. "I, well, I respect writers."

"But not actors."

"I didn't say that—"

"Let's not play this game anymore, shall we?" said Richard with a sigh.

They lapsed into silence. The air between them felt suddenly electric. Bree could feel the hair at the back of her neck rising with excitement and anticipation.

Anticipation of what? she wondered. She fidgeted as her mind drifted back to the two movies they'd seen that evening. Spencer Tracy and Katharine Hepburn: Bree had always thought them an unlikely pair, but now—yes, she'd noticed that "spark" that ignited between them on the screen. But then, they were both very good actors—

"Why don't people wear hats anymore?" said Richard, interrupting her silent thoughts.

Bree gazed at him. She shrugged her shoulders. "Nowadays, people dress more for comfort, I guess."

Richard smiled, his teeth flashing predatorially white in the moonlight. "Really?" His eyes wandered to her dress, taking in her stockinged feet, the shoes casually tossed to the side of the blanket.

"Well." Bree's hand moved to the bodice of her cream dress self-consciously. She gnawed on her lip for a moment before beginning to explain. "You see, before I—"

Richard suddenly leaned over, cupped her chin gently, and kissed her. Bree closed her eyes and let his lips linger over her mouth. He touched her hair, and traced the outline of her cheek with his fingers.

"Elephant shoes," he murmured throatily and kissed her again, more forcefully this time.

Bree slipped her arms about his shoulders and melted into the leathery smell of him. She cradled his head, running her fingers through his hair. But her sleeve had caught on a branch, causing a loud ripping sound. Attempting to undo the sleeve, the sudden motion brought Bree crashing forward, and she fell with a thud on top of him. Her chin struck his nose and a loud "OW!," accompanied by the sound of tearing fabric, wrenched through the peaceful night.

They lay there for a brief moment, perfectly still, their breaths ragged. They stared at each other. Richard's face suddenly crumpled into a loud wheezing laugh. Bree grinned and snorted, slowly pulling herself up. She squeezed her eyes shut, not daring to look down at her dress.

"Mrs. H is going to kill me!"

Richard cupped his nose. "Never mind your dress. What about my nose!" he complained nasally. "I'll never be able to work in show business again!"

Bree grimaced and looked contrite. "Oooh. I'm sorry. Is it bad? Let me see." She gently pried his hand away and looked at his nose. "I can't really see it in this light. Does it hurt?"

Richard pulled her head down and kissed her. "Not now, it doesn't." He nuzzled her neck, breathing in the fresh scent of her hair. Another r-r-rip! sliced the air.

The Camera-Shy Cupid

"Uh-oh. Now I'm definitely dead meat," Bree wailed, her hands coming up to cover her face in dismay.

Richard drew himself up on his knees, surveying the damage. His disheveled hair formed a lit halo about his head as he grinned faintly. "Gee, I could get arrested for this."

Bree sat up, lifted her right arm and poked the gaping tear in the cotton serge beneath the armpit. She noted the side slit in the skirt had lengthened up her thigh.

"Hey, I kind of like that," said Richard huskily, staring at her shapely leg.

Bree kneaded her brow, and tried unsuccessfully to amend the damage. But the damage was done. "Maybe you should take me home," she said, rising unsteadily to her feet. "While I still have some clothes left." She shivered as a breeze swept through the open back of her dress.

"Who designed this dress, anyway? The Keystone Kops?" Richard growled beneath his breath. "What is it with you and clothes?" He shook his head, a slow grin spreading across his face. Amusement shone in his eyes. "And here I thought you were a jeans and sweatshirt kind of girl."

I am, thought Bree, wearily. "Can we just go home?"

"Mine or yours?" He waved a dismissive hand before she could answer. "No, no. I take that back. My etchings aren't ready for you yet."

Yet? she echoed in a silent harrumph. But her face flushed nonetheless, and her fingers went to her lips, feeling the warm memory of his mouth on hers still lingering there. Bree drew in a deep breath and smoothed out the rumples in her dress, trying to muster up some sense of dignity.

"Here. Put this on." Richard draped his leather jacket over her shoulders.

Bree trembled slightly as she slipped her arms inside.

It hung loosely, the sleeves reaching almost to her fingertips. But she felt snug and warm, and safe—and suddenly very close to this man. She glanced up at him, and watched as he rolled up the blanket and screwed on the cap of the Coke bottle. She wanted to say something, something to ease the sudden awkwardness that had crept between them. They were the unuttered words, their thoughts and feelings shielded from each other. But strangely enough, the only words her mind could muster were "elephant shoes." So she bit her lip and said nothing.

They sped off down the gravel road, with Bree hanging on tightly, aware of her hands pressing into Richard's warm body. Her head reeled from the scent of him, and for a moment she felt lost as she closed her eyes and leaned her cheek into the small of his back.

"You okay?" he shouted, turning his head slightly.

She snapped open her eyes and stiffened. "Yes—yes. I'm okay." *You're swooning, Bree; get a grip. You can't fall for this guy,* she chastised herself.

Richard slowed as they neared her apartment building. He swung the bike up into the parking lot, but at the last minute swerved short of the front entrance and halted in the space next to her old green Rabbit. Bree glimpsed Mr. Braxton's stooping silhouette on the front steps.

"Uh, thanks—thanks for the pizza . . . and everything," she said, handing him back his leather jacket and helmet.

Richard climbed off the bike. His eyes glistened in the dim shadows cast by the building's entrance lights, and he took a step toward her.

"I'm sorry about your dress. . . ." His voice trailed clumsily as he glanced down at the helmet in his hand.

"That's okay," said Bree quickly.

Richard looked at her, and she could see his brow fur-

The Camera-Shy Cupid

rowing, his lips tightening into a sudden pensive frown. "Well," he said finally, "I guess I'd better let you go. Don't want you to catch cold. Tomorrow we have—" He paused. His face broke out into a slow grin.

Our kissing scene, Bree silently finished his sentence. She nodded and turned to leave.

"Bree? You, er, looked nice tonight," he said suddenly. "I had fun—well, considering." He gestured to her torn dress with an apologetic grimace.

"I had fun, too, Richard. I'll see you tomorrow."

"Elephant shoes," he answered with a grin.

Bree gave a small, puzzled laugh. "Uh, yes, elephant shoes."

She strode toward the triplex entrance, conscious of Richard's eyes following her. She could hear him whistling cheerily the theme song from *Adam's Rib*: "Farewell, Amanda." She grinned a grin that remained on her lips even as she waved to Mr. Braxton on the front stoop, and bounded up the steps, two at a time, to her apartment. Only when she was inside did her expression change as she caught her reflection in the mirror.

Her red curls sprang out about her head in a wild Raggedy Ann-like halo. Beneath her gray eyes, like a weary football player, semicircle smudges of mascara ran down her cheeks. She grimaced at herself and noticed with horror a piece of green olive wedged between her bottom teeth.

Bree! You look terrible! She picked at the piece of olive and ran her tongue over her teeth with dismay. But as she tramped off to the bathroom, she found herself suddenly breaking into happy song:

"Farewell, Ama-anda . . . *Adiós, adio, adieu . . .*"

Chapter Nine

Bree nodded, half-listening to Susanne Wayne explain the scene to her.

All morning she'd been trying to get that song out of her head. She floated about her apartment aimlessly, marking time before she would have to be on the set that afternoon. She forced herself not to think about last night, trying to quell her excitement and anticipation of seeing Richard again. Yet, even as she washed the dishes, ran the vacuum cleaner idly over the hall rug, absently picked up her laundry strewn about the apartment, she would find her thoughts drifting, and all of a sudden her heart would do a little tricky tumble, and perform a little tap dance behind her rib cage.

But now, as Susanne Wayne prattled on, her eyes swept about the hotel set nervously. She fidgeted, attempting to assuage the anxious knot in the pit of her stomach. Where was Richard?

The Camera-Shy Cupid

"Five minutes, everyone!" a woman with a headset called out.

"You'll do fine, Bree. Just give us what you showed us the other day." The pudgy producer gave her hand a reassuring squeeze and winked. She acknowledged the director's signal and waddled across the room.

"But Richard's not—"

And then, out of the corner of her eye, she saw him. Richard was standing, partially obscured beneath the leafy branches of a giant false castor oil tree at the other end of the hotel lobby set. He was watching her, a studious expression on his face. It changed into a brief fleeting smile as their eyes met. Bree fought down an impulse to wave, trying to keep her own smile from surfacing. She felt her neck suddenly grow hot, and a warm flush seeped into her cheeks. She began to make a beckoning gesture—what-are-you-doing-way-over-there?—then suddenly recalled the scene they were about to play out. No, he was, in fact, standing in the proper place. She closed her eyes, struggling to remember the lines of the script. But her mind blanked. *Come on, Bree. Concentrate.*

"Miss Gaston? Is everything all right?" a man in a headset frowned with concern.

She looked at him, and pressed the heel of her hand into her stomach. She exhaled, managing a faint smile. "Yes. Yes, I'm fine." However, at that moment her stomach did a quick handspring and she felt suddenly as though she might throw up.

From the far side of the room Richard's brows rose questioningly, his lips quirking into a boyish smile. Nervous? his mocking expression seemed to say.

Bree pursed her lips into what she hoped was an indifferent smile. With a toss of her hair, she lifted her chin resolutely and squared her shoulders confidently as she met his gaze.

"Sting Like a Bee" 's theme music drifted in and ebbed with a subtle gesticulation from the man in the sound booth.

Okay, don't mess up, Bree.

But much to her surprise, the scene unraveled perfectly, their lines delivered with the spontaneity and sincerity of Tracy and Hepburn. They moved, as if mesmerized by each other, into each other's arms. Their lips locked, Richard's hand cradling her head as Bree's arms came up to circle his neck. The walls of the room dissolved about them, and they were in that moment swept into another time and place. And so engaged in the embrace were they that they failed to hear the director's abrupt *"Cut!"*

That is, not until the crew broke out into a loud applause, hooting and whistling their appreciation.

Bree and Richard broke from their kiss and glanced about them. For a brief instant they were surprised and astonished by the presence of the other people. Bree's face flamed. But Richard grinned at her smugly and performed a comical bow on behalf of their audience, apparently undaunted, and even somewhat pleased by the crew's applause. Bree could feel her face redden now with frustration and anger.

"Now *that* was a kiss!"

But Bree turned deliberately and stalked off to the wardrobe room before he could finish. Sandy Masterson strode in, seconds behind her.

"That was quite a scene," she said, dazzling Bree with a healthy, white-toothed smile. "Richard's a great kisser, isn't he? But then, he's had a lot of practice."

Mrs. H emerged from the back with a grim expression. "What Bree needs is practice wearing expensive clothes." She shook her head and clicked her tongue.

"How you managed to ruin that dress, I can't imagine. Were you in some kind of wrestling match last night?" Her tone was scolding, but in her expression Bree could see she was genuinely perplexed.

"I, uh—" began Bree, wincing as she glanced over at Sandy.

The knock on the door was a welcome interruption. A woman with a clipboard poked her head in.

"Miss Gaston? Mr. Descartes would like a word with you before you leave."

Sandy raised her finely plucked brows. "Hobnobbing with the boss, I see."

Boss? Oh, yes. Philippe Descartes was, she supposed, the bankroll behind the Honey-Chew commercial project. Bree thought about how she'd stood him up last night. Well, not stood up exactly. But he certainly deserved a good excuse for her not dining with him at the Silver Chalice. Bree snarled to herself, thinking about Richard and that smug grin of his. She was an idiot, a fool.

Yes, that's what she'd tell Philippe.

Bree shrugged on her jeans and T-shirt. She'd meant to do laundry this morning, but naturally, the machines in her building had broken down again. She glanced at herself in the mirror, and with a Kleenex from her purse, she wiped off as much of the rouge and excess makeup as she could. The makeup man had insisted on decorating her eyes with that thick smudge-proof eyeliner that required a great deal of rubbing to take off. She gave up after a few minutes and sighed wearily at her reflection.

With her casual attire and the startling, made-up eyes, she looked half her age, a teenager playing the role of a grown up. She let out a small groan, wishing that for once she could exude at least a *little* sophistication.

Sandy's smile was wry, mocking. She took in Bree's rumpled appearance with a patronizing expression. "An off day?" she said with feigned sympathy. But Bree did not fail to detect the sneer in her voice.

Bree restrained a retort, and forced her lips into a smile. "I seem to be having a lot of those lately," she murmured. But this woman's condescending attitude was slowly managing to undercut her self-confidence, her blatant attractiveness making Bree feel all the more conscious of her own awkward youthfulness. She was beginning to see why Richard was interested in Sandy Masterson.

Oh, what do I care if he's attracted to her? And for that matter, why should I care what Sandy Masterson thinks of me? she thought, slinging her book bag over her shoulder. *Why let her play on my insecurities? You're a script reader, Bree,* she reminded herself. *Don't get caught up in all this glamor. You don't belong—*

Susanne Wayne opened the door and stuck her head in. "Bree! Fabulous job today. I'd like to have a little powwow with you sometime next week. We just received this wonderful new script, and we're all very excited about it. There's a part in it we'd like you to audition for, Bree."

New script? Ah, the Rudolph Gotham teleplay. "Uh, Miss Wayne, I don't—"

"We'll contact your agent. Zachary Chalmers, right?" She waggled her plump fingers. "Hello, Mrs. H!" She nodded to Sandy and closed the door behind her before Bree could finish her response.

"Everyone has their own technique, I suppose," said Sandy, fluffing up her bleached-blond hair. Her smile was thin as she turned to stare into the mirror. "Oh. Richard and I are going to the movies tonight—some old flick with, uh, Katharine Hepburn, I think—and, hmmm... what's his name? Travis? Traynor?"

"Tracy. Spencer Tracy," said Bree.

"Yes, that's it. But we're going to Cantonelli's right

now. You're welcome to come along, if you like." She batted her eyelashes, feigning a sudden forlorn look. "Oh! But you have a date with Philippe Descartes, don't you?"

"Date? No, uh, I think you have the wrong idea—"

"If you see Richard on your way out, tell him I'll be there in a couple of minutes. Thanks, Bree. You're a doll."

Bree paused in her step. "Uh, yes. Sure." She waved to Mrs. H, who sat on a stool in the corner of the narrow room, busy pinning the cuff of a blouse.

"I'm really sorry about the dress, Mrs. H. I'll pay for it as soon as I get paid."

"It's not beyond repair, dear."

"Let me pay for the repairs, at least. I know you have enough to do around here."

Mrs. H let out a long-suffering sigh, the wrinkles in her kindly face seeming to deepen all of a sudden. "Now isn't that the truth."

Bree exited and followed the arrows to the end of the hallway. As she rounded the corner she ran into Richard.

"Well, fancy meeting you, partner." He grinned.

"Partner, indeed," grumbled Bree. She gave him a perfunctory smile. "Sandy'll be out in a minute."

Richard gazed at her, his eyebrows raising slightly as he took in her old rumpled jeans and T-shirt. "Where're you off to in such a hurry?"

And Bree realized that she had indeed been moving with some haste.

"There you are, Mademoiselle Gaston."

Bree whirled around to spot Philippe Descartes strolling down the corridor behind her.

He smiled politely at Richard. "Monsieur Bell. I must congratulate you on your performance today." He turned to Bree with a nod. "Both of you were wonderful."

"It wasn't difficult. Bree makes it easy," said Richard,

slipping his arm possessively about her shoulders. "She's a natural."

"Yes, I can see that." Philippe's dark eyes gleamed a little as he gazed at Bree. He touched his chin, tilting his head to one side. "I'm sorry you could not make our dinner date last night. I trust you are well?"

Bree flushed, aware of Richard's sudden curious gaze. His hand fell from her shoulder. "Oh, yes. I'm fine. Unfortunately, something—something came up last night."

Richard's lips curved into an almost devilish smile.

Bree shot him a withering look, her teeth clenched.

But Philippe appeared not to notice their exchange. He smiled solicitously at Bree. "Perhaps we can reschedule for this evening, then?"

"Tonight? Well . . ." *I don't have anything to wear! Please, not the Silver Chalice—*

"In anticipation of your response I have already made reservations for seven o'clock this evening at the Silver Chalice."

"I think Bree's busy tonight," Richard blurted. He turned to her. "Right?"

Bree frowned. "What? No, no. I'm free."

"Wonderful!" said Philippe, his broad smile lighting up his handsome *GQ* face. Then he furrowed his brow, an equally attractive expression. "I am very pleased, because, unfortunately, I must return to Paris tomorrow. Alas, business," he added with a sigh.

"They don't serve pizza at the Silver Chalice, do they?" said Richard, unsmiling.

Bree ignored him. She smiled demurely at the Frenchman. "I would be honored to have dinner with you this evening, Mr. Des—*Philippe.*"

"It is I who am honored, Mademoiselle Gaston." He swept up her hand and brushed his lips along her knuckles; a ludicrous gesture had it been done by anyone else.

The Camera-Shy Cupid 121

But with Philippe Descartes, this kind of outdated behavior seemed all too appropriate.

"Please, call me Bree."

"Bree." He smiled. "I shall call for you, then, at . . . six-thirty?"

"Uh, I'll meet you there. Is that all right?"

Richard's brows shot up.

Philippe's smile wavered slightly. And then in the same instant he gave a low laugh, a husky sound that was pleasing to the ear. His dark eyes twinkled. "An independent woman. Ah, you are most interesting, Bree Gaston. I look forward to getting to know you better."

Bree flushed.

"Well, if you'll excuse me, I have a date of my own," said Richard with a curt nod of his head. "Have fun, you two." And he strode past them, heading back toward the wardrobe room.

Bree watched him, gnawing on her lip. There had been something in Richard's voice, a tightness, something that made Bree draw back. It was almost as if he were— Was Richard . . . angry?

"I shall see you at seven o'clock, then?"

Bree reverted her attention to the man standing before her. "Oh, yes. Seven." She nodded.

In the taxi on the way home, she mentally went through her wardrobe. She really didn't have anything appropriate to wear to a place like the Silver Chalice. She rubbed her temples. Certainly she couldn't just walk in there wearing one of her old $39.95 dresses. And asking Mrs. H to lend her another outfit—after what happened to that beautiful cream serge dress—wasn't such a hot idea. Oh, why had she accepted Philippe Descartes's invitation?

But she knew why. It had been that smug grin on Richard's face. What nerve. Did he really think that she'd go out with him once and immediately fall in love with him?

Besides, he and Sandy were going out tonight, weren't they? And he had the gall to invite her to see the Tracy and Hepburn double feature. He would probably take her up to "Inspiration Point" later this evening—

Wait a second! She was beginning to sound like a jealous girlfriend. She couldn't be *jealous,* could she? No, of course not, and she immediately dismissed the thought.

She tapped the driver's shoulder and told him to change course and head downtown to Cunningham's. As she sat back, massaging her neck, she realized that in accepting Philippe Descartes's dinner invitation this evening, she had, in truth, meant to make *Richard* jealous.

She fished in her book bag for her credit card and sighed. This new acting job was turning out to be more expensive than she liked.

"Ah, Mademoiselle Bree, I am indeed the envy of all the men tonight," said Philippe, leaning forward to touch her hand.

"Thank you." Bree smiled uncomfortably.

The dress she'd bought at Cunningham's was a shade of jewel green that brought out the red highlights in her hair. But she wondered if the low scooped neck was appropriate. Bree was thinking, too, that she'd misjudged the practicality of the dress she'd bought; for when she'd sat down, the snugness of the green material did not stretch at all, but cramped her legs together under the table. There was no way, this evening, that she'd be comfortable.

What could I have been thinking? she thought grimly. *Who was I trying to impress?*

But she could see that Philippe Descartes was impressed. She shied self-consciously under his approving gaze, but at the same time she felt a little thrill of exhilaration shiver through her. His look made her feel vibrant,

The Camera-Shy Cupid 123

and a little proud—as if she were, indeed, the most beautiful woman sitting in this extravagantly posh restaurant.

But the place did make her ill at ease, and she found herself chatting away about nothing to compensate for her nervousness. *Shut up,* she scolded herself. *He's going to think you're a bubblehead.*

And then there was the matter of the menu. Strangely enough, it was all in French.

Philippe watched her. He seemed not to notice the female attention his presence was attracting from the adjacent tables. "Forgive me. You see, they know me here, and automatically bring me the French menu. It was presumptuous of me to think you spoke French."

See? He already thinks you're a bubblehead. Bree reached for her champagne and took a long drink.

"I thought to myself: 'Bree Gaston'—a French name." He laughed, a light, cheery sound. And there was no note of condescension in his words, but oddly enough, a hint of relief. "So many women I meet put on, well, masks, as you might say. They pretend to be someone they are not." He poured more champagne into her glass. "But you, you are your own person, I can see this. I admire this quality in you. You are—" He touched his chin, musing for a moment. "You are intriguing."

Oh, I'm intriguing, all right. Bree took another sip of her champagne, feeling the sweet, cool liquid slowly wash away her tension. *Don't get drunk,* a voice in the back of her mind warned.

"Well, I know a little French," she found herself saying. "Uh, let's see . . . *Marchez la fenêtre*—"

"Walk the window?"

"Oh, no. Well, I know the verbs. *Je suis, tu es, il est, nous,* uh—*nous sommes, vous*—"

"*Vous êtes ravissante ce soir,*" said Philippe, smiling.

"Let's see . . . 'you are,' uh—"

"Ravishing tonight."

"Your English is much better than my French," admitted Bree. Her head was buzzing like a doorbell, and her cheeks felt swollen with heat. *Better ease up on the champagne,* she advised herself.

"Perhaps I could teach you French sometime?"

"I'd like that." What? Why'd she go and say that? *Are you crazy? You barely passed French in junior high.*

Bree let Philippe order the meal. Most of the French spoken between him and the waiter went over her head, but the word "grenouille" immediately jumped out at her, making her suddenly cringe and pale in her seat. She'd learned that word in junior high: frog.

Though she was not normally queasy, nor ignorant of exotic foods, there were certain repasts Bree did not find particularly appetizing—frogs' legs being one of them.

"The snails are wonderful here," Philippe informed her.

Snails were another.

Bree took a sip of her champagne, hoping that her sudden unease didn't show.

Thankfully, Philippe took control of the conversation, moving Bree into the role of the listener who was required only to nod intermittently, maintain eye contact, and look interested. She thought about the scenes in the restaurant set of "The Camera-Shy Cupid," and wondered what Philippe's response would be if she muttered the occasional "cantaloupe" or "watermelon," or Richard's particular favorite, "elephant shoes." She chuckled to herself. *Ah, the occupational hazards of being an extra.*

". . . what is it? A script consultant?"

Bree snapped out of her reverie. "What? Oh, yes—er, no. No, I'm just a script reader, actually."

The Camera-Shy Cupid

Philippe regarded her as if he didn't understand her. "And you have been acting, for... how long?"

"Me?" *Five days.* "Uh, not long. I sort of got... pushed into it," she said, recalling George Kane's magnanimous entrance into her life.

"Discovered by George Kane. Yes, I have heard this." Philippe nodded. "A competent director." His darkbrown eyes sparkled like the champagne bubbles in their glasses. The corners of his mouth tipped up into a smile. "And a man of exquisite taste."

Bree flushed, partly from the compliment, partly from the champagne that was beginning to fuzz her thoughts.

"Perhaps you would like to accompany me to Paris this weekend?"

Bree choked back a small gasp of surprise. "Paris?"

"Yes. I would very much like to take you there—to show you around the city," he said. "That is, if you are free this weekend."

"Well, I don't know. I have a few things I need to—" Paris? The idea of her flying over to Paris for the weekend, with this man who looked like he should be gracing the cover of *The World's Most Beautiful* magazine, seemed all too unreal to her. Besides that— "Philippe, I hardly know you," she told him. But she'd always dreamed of one day going to Paris—

"Yes, I understand," said Philippe, looking visibly disappointed. "Perhaps after we finish the Honey-Chew campaign, then? I promise you will have a most wonderful time in my city. I am an excellent guide." He flashed his teeth.

Bree nodded, the slight gesture making her feel all the more light-headed and buoyant. *Careful, Bree,* she warned.

The waiter approached wheeling a trolley laden with select dishes of food trapped by chrome lids made to resemble the restaurant's castlelike turrets outside. With great care—Bree was wondering if perhaps a drum roll might start up somewhere in the background—the waiter unveiled the aperitifs.

Bree gazed down at the snail shells sunk into the tiny holes. *Like dirty golfballs,* she thought, feeling her throat constrict. Her eyes wandered to the basket of freshly cut bread, then watched as the waiter placed another dish next to the escargots.

"Escargots et cuisses de grenouille," ululated the waiter proudly. He spotted the nearly spent champagne bottle resting in the bucket on its side. *"Encore du champagne, Monsieur Descartes?"*

Philippe flourished a gesture with his hand, a surreptitious signal to the waiter, and the man bowed, turning to smile at Bree.

"Mademoiselle Gaston, vous aimez bien la champagne? Voulez-vous une autre bouteille?"

Bree smiled, not knowing what he was saying. So she simply nodded, making a noise in her throat to indicate that she was hungry and that the food looked good.

Philippe leaned forward confidentially. "You may order another year if you like. I thought this one a little sweet, but you seem to be enjoying it."

Oh, the champagne. "Oh, no. This year is fine." She smiled at the waiter hovering over the table. *"Uh, bonne année, oui?"* she said, nodding enthusiastically.

"Oui, mademoiselle," replied the waiter. His deferential tone was a practiced one for Americans who tried to speak French.

"Ah, it is rare to find an American restaurant that does not butcher escargots. I find so few chefs here are able to cook snails properly. Sometimes I think they collect the snails from their own gardens." Philippe laughed. "Can you imagine that?"

"Yes," muttered Bree, "imagine that."

Bree watched Philippe begin his operation on the snail. Wielding a forcepslike utensil, he scooped the shell out onto his plate. He then proceded to pry out the shriveled snail meat with a tiny two-pronged fork. Bree saw him tear off a morsel of bread, fold the cooked snail inside, and pop it into his mouth. She averted her eyes as he glanced over, and set out to imitate his procedure.

The shell escaped the clinches of her forceps and rolled over the rim of the plate. She hastily picked it up with her fingers, and stabbed it with her little fork. The meat came out easily, too easily, however, and it slipped off the fork tines and landed in the basket of bread. Bree grimaced determinedly, and fighting back her embarrassment, snagged it with a large piece of bread as if it were about to run away.

Philippe grinned, paying no heed to the disapproving glances from the next table.

With a deep breath, Bree bit into the bread. She felt the resistance of the rubbery meat between her teeth, and to conceal her disgust, she shoved the entire piece of bread into her mouth.

Philippe blinked. He cocked his head in curious amusement as Bree struggled to chew the large morsel.

"You have a big appetite. So many women these days do not eat," he said, evidently pleased. "Always they are dieting, nibbling food like little mice. They are afraid to enjoy what is important in this life."

Bree swallowed, pressed her lips together, and reached for her champagne. She drained it in one gulp. And in that moment, the waiter suddenly appeared, as if on cue, his smile deferential and solicitous.

He presented the new bottle to Philippe, who inspected it with a diligent eye. Philippe nodded, and the waiter popped the cork while another liveried waiter poured the remaining champagne into Bree's glass. All this was done with a perfunctory swiftness that left Bree breathless.

After tackling two more of the snails, the bread basket was empty.

"You seem to like bread," remarked Philippe.

"Yes, uh, I'm a bread person," replied Bree. She purposely avoided looking at the frogs' legs, eyeing the empty breadbasket uneasily; there was no way she was eating any more snails without bread, and she didn't even want to think about the frogs' legs at the moment.

As if reading her mind, the waiter reappeared and replaced the basket with another full one. Bree smiled at him gratefully, and he bowed. Philippe made a gesture with his hand, and the waiter paused, turning to her.

"Mademoiselle Gaston is finished?"

The unfamiliar use of her name rattled her. She blinked and nodded. "Thank you. It-it was wonderful."

He cleared the table, leaving behind the fresh basket of bread.

Philippe indicated the basket. "Please, eat. It is good bread."

Bree smiled politely. "Yes, uh, it is good." And she reached for another slice and bit into it. She could feel her stomach expanding against the unstretchability of her dress with every bite. *I can't eat any more,* she thought in silent distress. But she managed to swallow down the morsel, and then, under Philippe's urging, watchful eye, she ate another.

By the time the main course, steak tartare, was served, Bree had polished off the bread and was ready to bust out of her dress. The champagne was making her giddy, and she suspected, from the looks she was getting from nearby tables, that she was talking a little too loud. She'd expected the bread to have a cushioning effect on the alcohol. Apparently, she was wrong.

The Camera-Shy Cupid 129

The room spun about her like a merry-go-round, and she realized that she was the only passenger. She squinted at Philippe, who was asking her something.

"... you and Richard Bell?"

"Richard?" Bree tried to focus her eyes on Philippe's face. "Oh, there's nothing between Richard and me," she said with a little too much vehemence.

Philippe frowned. "I was asking if Zachary Chalmers was representing both of you."

"Oh."

"But I am delighted to hear the two of you are not romantically involved," said Philippe, resting his hand on hers. "I admit that after seeing you two together at the suite, and then at the studio—"

"That was only *acting*," said Bree, surprised at the bitterness in her tone.

Philippe leaned forward, his dark eyes slowly roaming over her. "I wish I was your acting partner," he said huskily.

Acting partner. Yes, she supposed that's what Richard was to her. They worked together, that was all. But in her mind she was feeling his soft lips pressing against her own, his hands about her waist. And for one brief instant she thought she caught a whiff of his leathery scent. She felt herself swooning.

Philippe's hand enclosed hers tightly. "Bree? Are you all right?"

Bree gazed up at him with a rueful smile and pressed her palm to her forehead. "A little too much champagne, I'm afraid." She managed to straighten in her chair, but the room was moving too fast. "Do you mind if we—?"

"Of course. I shall take you home." He beckoned to the waiter, performing a subtle series of finger gestures as if the man were deaf.

The limousine was waiting outside, and Bree climbed

in, paying no mind to her dress twisting up past her knees—or her shoe, which fell onto the pavement. Philippe retrieved it and emitted a small laugh as Bree stared curiously at her stockinged feet.

"My Cinderella," muttered Philippe. He slipped it on her foot.

"It fits." Bree giggled. *You're tipsy!* scolded the voice in the back of her mind. But the evening's champagne had already taken effect, and she leaned her head back against the black leather seat with a happy, weary sigh.

"Where do you live, Bree?"

Bree envisioned the limousine pulling up in front of her triplex, and Mr. Braxton stepping off the stoop to greet Philippe with his empty whiskey bottle. Philippe would come up to her apartment and trip over the laundry basket—

"One thirty-three Windhaven Road," she found herself saying.

Philippe relayed this to the driver, then closed the partition.

"Champagne doesn't usually do this to me," Bree attempted to explain. The truth was, the last time she'd drunk champagne was two years ago at a New Year's Eve party where she'd spent the majority of the evening with a splitting headache.

"No need to explain," said Philippe kindly. "I enjoyed our evening very much, Bree."

Nausea gripped her, and she pursed her lips, swallowing. But the feeling quickly dissipated, and she managed a weak nod. "Yes." Her head reeled. "I had a wonderful time, Mr. Des—Philippe."

"I'd like to see you again, Bree."

"You would?"

Philippe laughed. "Ah, Bree. You don't hide behind

The Camera-Shy Cupid 131

any... masks. You are so refreshing." He stroked her hair. "And so very beautiful."

If Bree wasn't feeling so giddy she would have blushed. But as it so happened, all she could do was squint at him out of one eye.

"And I meant it when I said I wanted to take you back with me to Paris." He brushed her cheek with the back of his hand, and inched closer so that their legs touched.

"Philippe—" began Bree.

The limousine halted, and Bree gazed out at the dark red-brick house. Lights shone from one of the upper Cape Cod windows. A car was parked in the driveway.

"Whose—?" Bree stopped herself as she suddenly recognized the house. She peered up at the windows, watching with suspense for the silhouetted figures to appear.

Philippe followed her gaze, curious. "You live here alone?"

"Alone? Oh, yes I live—"

Murphy's bark sounded from inside.

"With my dog."

"Oh? I like dogs. May I come in and meet him? Perhaps we could have a nightcap." Bree swayed slightly. "Or I could make you some coffee?"

Bree scrabbled for the door handle, found it, and yanked it open. Murphy's barking was going to wake up the entire neighborhood if she didn't get Philippe out of here. And her stomach was feeling a little queasy again.

"I'm sorry, Philippe. I have to go—"

"I'll walk you to your door."

"No! I mean, no. Uh, Murphy—my dog? He's not really great with strangers. Liable to bite your head off."

Philippe shrank back uncertainly. "Oh? Well, perhaps I'll wait here until you're safely inside."

"No, no. Go on. The longer you're here, the more Murphy'll bark. And I don't want to wake up the neighbors." *If they're not already awake*, she thought, swaggering a little. She moved to shut the door when Philippe suddenly climbed out, reached down, and kissed her on the lips.

"Bon soir, ma chérie, Cinderella." He smiled and sank into the back of the limousine.

Bree watched, unsteadily, as it veered back down the road from where it came.

The side door light flickered on, and the screen door opened. A man's head popped out and gazed at Bree.

"Who's there?"

Bree tiptoed toward him and stepped into the light. She grinned broadly. "Hi, Zachary. It's me."

Chapter Ten

It took Bree a moment to realize that the ringing in her ear wasn't a dream, but the telephone by her bed. She groaned and reached over to grab it.

"Hello?" she answered hoarsely.

"Well, I guess you had a good time last night."

Bree recognized Richard's voice. "Why are you calling me at..." She glanced over at her digital alarm clock, "...eleven-thirty?"

"So I gather you and Mr. French Adonis did the town last night? You sound hung over."

"I am not hung over," retorted Bree, cringing as a sharp, searing pain stabbed behind her eyes.

"Good. You're supposed to be at the 'Sting Like a Bee' studio in, uh, let's see... forty-three minutes."

"What?!"

"They called me this morning. Susanne Wayne needs us to finish up a small scene. Nothing major."

Bree groaned. "And you're calling me *now?*"

"Hey, I tried earlier, but neither you nor Mr. French Philosopher, there, would answer."

"French Philosopher—?" Bree glared at the receiver. "Philippe Descartes is not here!"

But her response was an even dial tone. She slammed the phone into the cradle and it fell crashing to the floor. This sudden violent motion brought a new stab of pain that began at the base of her neck and climbed all the way to the front of her brow. Bree thought that if she pulled on her ears her skull might crack open.

The phone rang again and Bree snatched it up.

"What?" she barked.

"Hey, is that any way to greet the guy who was kind enough to take you into his kitchen, ply you with coffee, and listen to you babble till two in the morning?"

"I was babbling?" Bree's heart did a two-step. She tried to remember. "Uh, what exactly was I babbling about?"

"I don't know—strange stuff. You seemed awfully mad about something. I just let you rant and rave."

Bree groaned loudly. "Aw, Zachary, I'm really sorry about that. I drank a lot of champagne last night." She rubbed her eyes, yawning. "Thanks for taking me home. I appreciate it."

"Yeah, well, that must have been some date you had last night. This place is turning into a lousy greenhouse."

"Huh? Greenhouse? I don't understand."

"It started early this morning. Flowers, huge bouquets of them. Funeral parlors don't have this many flowers." Zachary sneezed. "Rachel is in her glory, but she's starting to become suspicious—especially after she let the baker inside. We now have seven loaves of French bread in our freezer. We didn't know what to make of it, that is, until we came across the note."

"What note? Zachary, what are you talking about?"

The Camera-Shy Cupid

"You want me to read it? Here. I have the card right here in my hand: 'Thinking of you, my Cinderella,' " he read, "and it's signed: 'Your prince, Philippe.' " Zachary blew his nose. "So I put two and two together and figured you and Philippe Descartes were playing fairy tale last night. Only I don't remember Cinderella ever getting drunk. Hey, this thing with you and Philippe, it sounds almost serious. Could it be—"

"Zachary," Bree warned over the phone.

"Okay, okay. I won't pry. Anyway, I've been trying to reach you. Susanne Wayne contacted me this morning—"

"Yes, I know. Richard just called me," grumbled Bree. "Zachary, if you're going to be my agent, you'd better start listening to me. Are you listening?"

"You don't have much time. You'd better get moving—"

"I don't want you to put me up for any more jobs. As soon as this Honey-Chew thing is over, I'm quitting. No walk-on, walk-off, walk-throughs, walk-whatever; no extra work, period. And definitely no romantic kissing scenes. I'm through with it, you hear? I'm throwing in the towel."

"That's great, Bree," said Zachary, "but you give me a little too much credit, I think. The truth is, I had no hand in getting you these jobs. The studios, they called *me*. I haven't even started soliciting for you."

"You make it sound so unsavory."

"Whatever. I heard they're looking for someone to play—"

"No. Absolutely not. I don't care what role is offered to me. I'm not taking it—and that's that."

Bree slumped against the studio wall with a weary sigh. "Thank goodness that's over with."

"Let me guess. Monsieur Advertising-Executive-From-Paris plied you with champagne and caviar all night," sneered Richard.

Try snails and frogs' legs, retorted Bree silently. *And bread.* She patted her stomach with a grimace. Who said man cannot survive on bread alone? Bread and champagne, that is.

A woman with a clipboard and headset approached from the end of the hall. Under her arm she carried a long thin package wrapped in blue-and-white tissue paper.

"This came for you this morning, Miss Gaston."

Bree stared at it.

"Well? Aren't you going to open it?" said Richard, peering curiously over her shoulder.

As she tugged at the tissue paper, a small square card fluttered to the floor. Richard bent down and picked it up.

" 'I'll be thinking about you as I pass the boulangerie here in Paris. Philippe,' " read Richard. His eyebrows shot up, then furrowed. Sarcasm tugged at the corner of his lips. "So why didn't he just take you with him to Paris?"

"Because I said no." Bree gazed at the French baguette in her hand and laughed.

"What? No pâté?" His smile was thin. "I guess you two really hit it off, huh?" He looked down at the baguette in her arms, his blue eyes frosting over suddenly. "Well, I'll see you later, then." And he walked away from her, his hands thrust deep in his tuxedo pockets.

She closed her eyes and groaned loudly. Her head throbbed, her stomach ached, and now a new heaviness fell with a resounding thump behind her ribs. She suddenly yearned to be back shuffling through the slush pile of scripts, sitting behind her old cubbyhole desk in the reading department, where the only excitement to be

The Camera-Shy Cupid 137

found was in the occasional well-written words of a teleplay.

"Ah! Good! You haven't left yet."

Bree opened her eyes and blinked at the smiling, fleshy face. "Sting Like a Bee" 's coproducer linked her arm in Bree's with a quiet, confidential motion.

"I've just contacted your agent, Bree. We'd like you to consider playing a part in this new script we're shooting next month. We're all very excited about it," said Susanne Wayne. Her tiny blue eyes were like two dazzling, deep-set opals. "All we're waiting for now is the author's release."

"This author—his name wouldn't happen to be . . . Rudolph Gotham?"

The producer gazed at her in surprise. "Why, yes. You've heard of him, then? I was under the impression the man was an unknown. We couldn't find any listing of him in the Screenwriters' Guild."

"I, uh, recommended that script."

Susanne Wayne's doubtful look quickly melted into sudden comprehension. She laughed. "Oh, but of course. I forgot you used to work in the script reading department."

I still do. "Listen, Mrs. Wayne—"

"Susanne. Bree, I'm sorry. Can this wait?" She sighed a suffering smile. "We're doing reshoots all day, and naturally, we're behind schedule. As always." She patted Bree's hand almost consolingly. "But we've already sent a copy of the script to your agent. Zachary Chalmers, isn't it?"

"Yes, but—"

Susanne Wayne flourished a frantic wave and toddled with a half-skip run down the corridor. "We'll be in contact soon!" she called back, her fat fingers waggling.

Bree stood for a moment in the empty hallway, clutching the French baguette to her chest like a rifle. She needed to talk to Zachary before this acting business swallowed her up. Yes, things were definitely getting out of hand.

"Okay, before you say anything, I think you should first take a look at this 'Camera-Shy Cupid' script," said Zachary quickly. He reached into the pile of papers on his desk and fished out a bound copy.

Bree glanced at the byline: Rudolph Gotham.

"Read it. It's hilarious. And the part Gail Sussmann picked out for you? It's you to a T. I mean really; it's almost as if the script were written with you in mind." He gestured with his hand. "Turn to the marked page and read the character description."

Bree read: *INT. RESTAURANT. Woman thirtyish, with long red curly hair, slim build, gray eyes—*

"Zachary!"

"Didn't I tell you? Almost spooky." He grinned. "And you wonder why they want *you* for the part."

Bree shook her head. "There must be other actresses who fit this description."

"Read it, and maybe you'll change your mind."

Bree gnawed on her lip. It was tempting. But who was she kidding? She wasn't an actress. The only reason she'd managed to get through that one speaking part on "Sting Like a Bee" was Richard. It had been Richard who'd steered her safely through, empowering her, somehow making her forget her self-consciousness. It was Richard who was the actor; she was just following his lead.

"Is there a part in this for Richard?" she asked, flipping through the script.

"Huh? Richard? You mean Richard Bell? I don't

know. I don't think so." Zachary frowned. "Does it matter?"

"Zachary, I don't—"

"Don't say no just yet. Take a few days to think about it." He suddenly gave an "Oh!," and fished out another script. He held it up, grinning from ear to ear. "Remember that 'Sting Like a Bee' script? The one you recommended? Well, guess who just landed a juicy role in it?"

Bree's shoulders sagged. "Aw, no. Not the Rudolph Gotham one." She groaned. "Susanne Wayne cornered me about that today." Bree mimed a *"YOU'RE OUT!"* signal, as an overenthusiastic baseball umpire might upon the player's third strike. "Forget it. I'd only ruin it, Zachary."

"But you should see what they're offering—"

"Money isn't the issue, here. Heaven knows how much I could use it—but I don't need it that badly," said Bree, shaking her head.

"But there are other things to consider . . . like success, fame—"

"Fame?" Bree laughed. "You know me, Zachary. I've never in my life wanted to be famous. That kind of thing doesn't interest me. I'm a script reader."

"Aw, Bree. You could be so much more," prompted Zachary.

"Then promote me to the editorial staff. No—" She hastily changed her mind. "Believe it or not, I *like* my old job in the reading department."

Zachary scratched his head and let out a breath of weary exasperation. "Okay, okay. I'll call Susanne Wayne. But what about 'The Camera-Shy Cupid'?"

"I'll finish my work as an extra, but that's it," she told him firmly. "I'm afraid you've just lost one of your clients."

Zachary shot her a reticent smile. "Well, at least all's not lost."

"What do you mean?"

"Oh. I didn't tell you, did I? Richard Bell called me up yesterday. I'm representing *him*, now."

Chapter Eleven

"Cantaloupe, watermelon."

"Raspberry, strawberry, boysenberry," answered Bree. "Potato, tomato, avocado."

For the past three days, this was what their low-key conversation had been reduced to: reciting vegetables and fruit on the restaurant set of "The Camera-Shy Cupid." It was an easy way to make a living, thought Bree; but her enthusiasm had gotten lost somewhere between the "cucumber" and the "cauliflower."

Across the table Richard smiled at her. But the twinkle had disappeared from his eyes, and he seemed to purposely distance himself from her. Bree managed to return his smile, but her dinner partner's change in attitude rankled her. She wondered at the gnawing ache in her chest, which seemed to only intensify as the scene continued. She wondered, too, why his sudden coolness bothered her so. Yet, she could not bring herself to ask him outright why he was acting this way, why all of a sudden this icy veneer. So instead, she simply followed his lead.

"Escargots, cuisses de grenouille," she muttered.

Richard gazed at her through lowered lashes. "Is that for the benefit of your boyfriend, over there?"

"Huh? What?"

"Don't tell me you didn't notice Mister *GQ*-from-Paris watching us."

"Philippe's here?"

After yesterday's shoot, she'd run into Philippe just as she was leaving. Penny Dowling was with him then, but he had abruptly excused himself from his conversation to go over and speak with Bree.

"We keep missing each other, it seems," he said. "Twice, I stopped by your home, yesterday. But your cleaning lady told me you'd just left."

"Cleaning lady?" Bree looked at him, puzzled.

"I cannot remember her name, now . . . Michelle? Danielle? No, it begins with an R, I think."

"Rachel?" Bree felt her tongue thicken.

"Rachel. Yes, I believe that is what she said her name was." He smiled, and a keen glint came into his dark brown eyes. "Alas, business prevents me from seeing you tonight." His voice lowered huskily. "And I would very much like to see you again, Bree."

He persuaded her to let him take her out for lunch at a quaint bistro nearby. His attentiveness flattered Bree. He listened to her, his dark eyes intense and alert, observing her with undisguised interest. Twice he had reached out to hold her hand, and she'd felt herself blushing uneasily under his warm touch. She was conscious of his startling handsomeness, and the charm that seemed to come so easily to him, had rendered her almost tongue-tied. For a brief instant as he clasped her hand in his, she thought

The Camera-Shy Cupid   143

she glimpsed Richard pass by the window. But when she turned to look, he wasn't there.

He had been asking her a question. "Bree?" Philippe prompted, following her gaze with a frown.

"Oh, I'm sorry. What were you saying?"

"I was asking if you'd like to see me tomorrow evening."

Bree could not remember her response, but she knew she had not said no.

Now, Philippe Descartes was here on the set waiting for her. She wondered at the strange mix of feelings suddenly churning inside her. For a brief, fleeting moment, as she gazed at the man sitting opposite her, she wished Philippe hadn't come. At the same time Bree found herself willing the restaurant scene to go on, if only to be with Richard for a few more minutes—

What are you saying? Have you gone crazy? Bree shook her head in wonderment. *You have one date with this guy, and you already think you're falling head over heels in love with him? Get real; you don't even know Richard Bell!*

And meanwhile there's this incredibly attractive, successful man who has obviously taken an interest in you, waiting and willing to take you away from all this—

"Goodness, Bree," Rachel had spoken to her over the phone. "This man is spending a fortune on you. I'm thinking of opening up my own flower shop—or bakery," she added with a laugh. "Rich and handsome and French. That's what I call a lethal combination. What are you waiting for, girl? Grab him before I do!"

What *was* she waiting for? Well, for one, there was the matter of that little lie—

"Your boyfriend taking you to the Silver Chalice again—or is he flying you out to Paris this time?" said

Richard, jarring her out of her reverie. He stuffed a french fry into his mouth.

"He's not my boyfriend," Bree retorted.

"Could have fooled me."

"I guess you're easily fooled, then," said Bree, forking her pasta.

"I'm a fool all right," he muttered under his breath.

Bree gazed at him, sucking air between her teeth. "Look, Philippe and I are just—" "Friends," she was about to say. But the man in the ripped jeans interrupted her.

"A-A-And cut! That's a wrap, folks!" Bree noticed the lettering stitched across the front of his T-shirt. It read: LENS BE FRIENDS. *This guy needs to see Mrs. H,* thought Bree. *And doesn't he have any jeans that* aren't *ripped?*

"See Bill for next week's casting schedule!" he yelled above the din. "For those of you who will still be with us, that is," he added, glancing over at Bree and Richard.

Richard rose from his chair, staring at her. "I heard you turned down the role on 'Sting Like a Bee,' " he said, frowning.

"Yes. It—I'm through with acting. No more. I'm finished after this job."

Richard cocked an eyebrow. "Not quite. We still have the Honey-Chew commercial—unless you've decided to bow out of that one, as well."

Bree sighed. "No. The contract's already signed." *And I need the money,* she sighed silently.

"And I suppose you're not going to take the role of Deanna, either." Richard seemed visibly frustrated.

"Deanna? Oh—you mean the guest character on 'The Camera-Shy Cupid.' " How'd he know about that? "No, I couldn't," she said, shaking her head. "That script is really good. I'd only ruin it."

"But that part was written for you," Richard blurted

The Camera-Shy Cupid 145

in protest. He immediately cringed and glanced away. His mouth worked silently as if to say something more, but he changed his mind and merely grimaced.

"I'm not sure I understand—"

Richard shoved his hands into his jeans pocket. "You better not keep Mr. French Ad Executive waiting." He glanced around the set moodily. "I guess I'll be seeing you on Monday, then."

"Monday?" Oh, yes, they were leaving for Grable on Monday to shoot the Honey-Chew commercials.

"Well, here comes your boyfriend."

"He's not my—"

"Hello, Bree." Philippe stood before them, elegantly attired in a soft blue Ralph Lauren shirt and jeans. He nodded to Richard. "How are you, Mr. Bell?"

"Great. Wonderful." Richard shook his hand. "Will you be joining us in Grable, Mr. Descartes?"

"Fortunately my schedule allows me this privilege," said Philippe, his dark eyes shifting to rest on Bree. Bree flushed under his penetrating gaze.

"Hmmm . . . yes, how fortunate," said Richard crisply.

Philippe's eyes narrowed for a brief instant. Then, as if to clear the air, he waved his hand in a brusque dismissive upward motion, and turned to Bree.

"I have two tickets for the symphony this evening," he said, smiling. "I would be most honored if you'd accompany me. That is, if you are free this evening."

"Uh, yes. That-that sounds lovely."

"I believe tonight it is Amir—" Philippe paused, frowning. "Now the name of the conductor escapes me."

"Kasdan. Amir Kasdan," Richard interjected with a cool smile.

"Yes, that's it. Are you a—how do you say?—a fan of classical music, Mr. Bell?" Philippe asked him.

"I've been to one or two concerts," Richard answered

offhandedly. "Well, have a good time." He shot a quick look at Bree before turning to wend his way about the tables. He walked briskly toward the exit where the other extras milled. Sandy Masterson broke away from a conversation and caught up with him, and they strode arm in arm out of the room.

"Shall I pick you up, then? Or would you prefer to meet me at my hotel suite?" He laughed. "Perhaps if I introduced myself to your dog, he and I could get to know each other better. And then maybe he would not get so upset by my presence."

Now's the time to tell him, thought Bree with grim resolution. She was thinking about all those flowers and loaves of bread filling up Zachary and Rachel's house. "I never thanked you for all those flowers... and the bread," she began hesitantly.

Philippe leaned a little closer. "I will admit I am charmed by your company, Bree. And I was hoping we might get to know each other better." He smiled, his dark eyes searching her face. His hand touched her shoulder. "Will you join me for dinner in my suite. Six o'clock?"

"In your suite?" Bree gnawed on her lip. "Um, well..."

"I'm staying at the Coriander Plaza."

Naturally—the Coriander Plaza was the most prestigious, the most expensive hotel in Boise.

"Okay," she said finally.

Philippe's face lit up. He reached for her hand, pausing to clasp it for a moment in both of his, then brought it to his lips. "I look forward to seeing you this evening, my sweet Cinderella."

Bree watched his confident stride take him across the room. She took in the way his head tilted up, the perfectly coiffed hair, the spotless, unwrinkled shirt and jeans that moved smoothly and in sync with the swinging of his

The Camera-Shy Cupid

limbs. Again she envisioned a sleek panther prowling through a jungle terrain. And indeed, before he reached the exit, he was ambushed by George Kane and Tom Bronfmann. Bree remarked the sudden rigidity of his body language, the expression on his handsome, lean face suddenly turning hard and businesslike.

Richard came in then, his light brown hair mussed from the helmet he carried tucked under his arm. He caught Bill from Casting's attention, and spoke to him, grinning. Bill shook his hand and patted him on the shoulder. They laughed, Richard's hearty guffaw sailing above the steady chatter in the room. He turned suddenly, and saw Bree staring at him. For a moment their gazes locked. Bree felt herself flush, and she lowered her eyes and retreated quickly into the narrow hallway. Her heart was thumping in her chest as she veered toward the wardrobe room.

She very nearly collided with Mrs. H as the elderly woman was in the process of locking the door.

"Well, child. You look in a state."

"I do?" Bree caught her breath. There was a giddiness in the pit of her stomach. *What's wrong with me?*

"You need something, Bree?"

Bree suddenly remembered. "Yes, as a matter of fact, I was wondering if I might borrow—"

"Ah, don't tell me, love," said Mrs. H, unlocking the door with a tired sigh. But her eyes crinkled at the corners and a motherly tenderness spread into her wrinkled face. "Which dress do you want to borrow this time?"

Despite her nervousness, the meal went without a hitch. The opulent surroundings of Philippe's suite had the look and feel of a tastefully decorated dining room, and Philippe, noting her look in that direction, had courteously closed the French doors leading to his bedroom suite. She sipped her wine, carefully monitoring her intake this time.

Under his watchful eye, she consumed the ample servings of bread with an exaggerated voraciousness that made her bloated stomach cry out in protest.

The warning bells clanging in her head abated as the evening wore on, and they relaxed into conversation. She listened idly as Philippe told her about his childhood in Nice, describing scenes from his years at the Sorbonne that led to the beginnings of his eventual involvement in the advertising business. At any other time, Bree would have found his anecdotes fascinating. But this evening she was feeling strangely restless. In her head, thoughts buzzed and eddied into a whirling haze, like a lens moving in and out of focus. Bree blinked in annoyance, and forced herself to pay attention to the conversation, leaning so far across the small table, a curly tendril of her hair trailed into the gravy boat.

"Oh," she said, pulling back abruptly.

"Wait, allow me." Philippe dipped his napkin into his water glass and came around to kneel beside her. He gently rubbed the brown milky substance from her hair. "So beautiful," he murmured throatily. And before Bree could thank him, he reached up and kissed her.

It was a long, tender kiss, and Bree liked it. At least she thought she did. Bree's hands came to rest on his shoulders as if she were steadying herself on the back of a chair. Philippe's fingers entwined the back of her neck. She closed her eyes and for a brief instant imagined Richard's shoulders, his leathery, manly smell, and Richard's lips—not Philippe's—pressing against hers.

Philippe released her slowly, a small, breathless smile playing on his lips. "I apologize. I startled you, I see."

Bree almost laughed. He hadn't startled her. If anything, that kiss had been telegraphed ten minutes before it happened. Strange, though, when she and Richard had played out that scripted love scene for the "Sting Like a

The Camera-Shy Cupid 149

Bee'' episode, yes—that time she'd been startled. No, not startled, exactly, but astonished, perhaps—

"Perhaps we had better be going." Philippe glanced at his Rolex. "The concert begins at eight."

"Yes," said Bree absently, collecting her purse.

"And then maybe after the concert we could come back here for—how you say?—a nightcap?" Philippe grinned at her. He ushered her through the door before she could respond.

As the lights dimmed over them, and the tall, thin figure of Amir Kasdan glided onto the stage, a great applause resonated through the concert stadium. Philippe inched closer to her, and Bree felt her back straighten in response, even as the orchestra opened with a magnanimous rendition of Rossini's *William Tell* Overture.

The fury of the strings spawned in her images of cowboys riding across the dry desert plains. And she could see the heads of the audience bobbing in time to the swift, galloping beat. Though Bree had been cautiously frugal with the wine this evening, she still felt inexplicably lightheaded and jumpy.

But as the evening wore on, the music began to set her mind and body adrift. Like a slow anesthetic, Tchaikovsky segued into Mozart's "Elvira Madigan," and the tension in Bree's shoulders melted away. With half-closed eyes, she let her thoughts wander, blocking out the presence of the audience, leaving for a moment the Gothic-inspired columned walls of the theater.

With the notes of the piano and strut of the cello, she imagined herself speeding along an unpaved road, the wind taking flight in her long red curls. Her arms were tightly entwined about a man's hard, muscled waist, and she breathed in the heady aroma of leather. Emotion roused within her, and her lips parted, then curved into a sudden smile. She saw Richard, his boyish grin—that wolfish, daredevil look in his eye. "Elephant shoes," he was whispering in her ear. Bree shivered with pleasure, and heard herself giggle aloud. She snapped open her eyes and put her hand to her mouth.

Next to her, Philippe gazed at her curiously, and Bree flushed, flashing him a tentative smile. He leaned closer so that their shoulders touched, and he reached for her hand. Bree scratched the back of her neck, staring straight ahead. Philippe moved his hand to his own lap.

Philippe did not veil his disappointment when Bree declined his invitation to join him for a nightcap in his hotel suite. But he was by no means ready to give up.

"You won't invite me in?" Philippe stood, craning his neck, trying to peer through the curtains of the side door.

Bree glanced at the limousine anxiously. Luckily, Zachary and Rachel were out for the evening, and Philippe seemed unaware of the fact that their Ford Taurus was conspicuously absent this time. Inside, Murphy was going crazy, barking and scratching at the door.

"I think you had better open the door before your dog breaks it down," suggested Philippe.

"Yes, uh, but I'm a little tired, Philippe—"

Headlights suddenly flashed behind them, and a car slowly rolled up into the driveway. The limousine's lights flickered on, and Bree and Philippe stared, dazed, like startled deer caught in the middle of the road. A head poked out of the car.

"Uh-oh."

"Hey, sorry!" A man's voice rang out. "Wrong house!"

Bree recognized Zachary's voice. She grimaced and let out a low groan. The car quickly reversed out of the driveway and sped down the road.

The Camera-Shy Cupid

"Now, that was odd," muttered Philippe.

"Not as odd as you think." Bree sighed under her breath. *You have to tell him; it's time you were honest with him—with yourself.* "Philippe, I have to tell you something—"

Philippe gestured to the limo driver, and the lights abruptly winked out. As the shadows of the evening folded over them again, Philippe grasped her waist gently and pulled her to him. "Bree, I haven't been able to stop thinking about you. It's been a long time since I've met a woman I feel I can trust, who is so... honest." He moved his face in closer. "And beautiful."

Bree put up her hand and his lips fell on her palm. "Philippe—"

Philippe released her, and put his finger to her lips. "No. No, I understand. You still need some time to get to know me." He straightened his bow tie, his eyes catching a gleam of moonlight. "Yes, of course. I am going too fast. I realize this. It is unfair of me to expect you to fall in love with me as I have fallen in love with you."

Fallen in love? With me? Bree blinked in astonishment. "But—but you hardly know me!"

"I know my heart; it does not lie."

Mine does. Bree winced inwardly. She looked down at her feet. She really was no Cinderella, and she had to let him know this. "Oh, Philippe."

Murphy whined behind the door as if in response.

Philippe touched her arm. "I will wait until you are safely inside. And then, tomorrow we will do something together. Yes? Perhaps go to the museum? I have heard that they have a wonderful photography exhibit this month." He smiled happily. "We could maybe have lunch together? I have a meeting in the morning, but the rest of my day is free."

"Well..."

"I am not leaving until you are safely inside." He grinned at her. "I want to make certain you are intact for our date tomorrow."

Bree gnawed on her lip, grimaced, and opened her purse, rummaging in pretense for the nonexistent keys. After a moment, she said in a meek voice: "I, uh, must have locked the keys inside."

"Oh? You don't have a spare?"

Bree glanced around in the dim light. She checked under the mat. No key. The flowerpot. Not there, either. She tried to think. In the mailbox? She moved along the side of the house and opened the old milk box door. Just some commercial flyers stuffed inside.

"Well, it appears as though you are locked out of your house," mused Philippe. "Perhaps this is a sign that you should come back with me—"

"It's not my house," Bree suddenly blurted out.

Philippe frowned. "I'm sorry. I thought you said—"

"I don't live here. This house, it belongs to my friend Zachary Chalmers."

"Your agent? I don't understand."

"I live on the other side of town in a dingy old one-bedroom apartment on Cranberry Street," Bree confessed without taking a breath.

Shadows hung ominously across Philippe's face. He stared at her, his eyes dewy and glittery in the moonlight, but very still. In the sudden silence that lapsed between them, Bree thought she heard Debussy's "Prelude à L'Après Midi d'une Faune" grumbling in the background. Someone had once told her jokingly that *faune* was, in fact, the French word for the Greek goddess Fauna. She was supposed to be the goddess of fertility, of animals and nature. Apparently, she was famous for her uncommon chastity after she was married. But to Bree, Debussy's prelude always sounded too eerie, almost

The Camera-Shy Cupid 153

Hitchcockian—a prelude to a husband contemplating strangling his wife because she had lied and given her heart away to another.

Bree frowned uneasily.

"I see," said Philippe finally. "You were afraid I would not fall in love with you if I knew the truth about where you lived." He took a step toward her, and Bree recoiled slightly. But he was smiling.

"Oh, Bree. Do you think I would care about something so trivial? It does not matter whether you live in a one-room apartment or a mansion. Don't you see? I am in love with you."

Bree kneaded her temples. "But Philippe," she said in a very small voice, "I-I think I'm in love with someone else."

Her eyes immediately snapped wide, momentarily stunned by her own blunt confession. She wanted to bite back what she had just said. But she knew in her heart that what she had just blurted out was true.

"Oh," was all Philippe said. His lips drew into a thin line, and the muscles in his cheeks twitched.

"I'm so sorry, Philippe. I didn't know—" *What do you mean you didn't know?*

Philippe adjusted his bow tie, stretched his neck right, then left, and threw back his shoulders. He ran his hands methodically down the sleeves of his jacket. "No, Bree. It's quite all right. I understand perfectly," he said, his tone very even and controlled. "I do hope your friends enjoyed the flowers and bread." Unmistakable hostility smoldered beneath these words, and Bree bit her lip, restraining herself from reaching out to him. His expression had grown estranged in the evening light. "Good night, Miss Gaston."

He walked back to the limousine and slammed the door. In a matter of seconds the limousine was tearing out of the driveway and squealing back down the road toward downtown.

A few minutes later, Zachary and Rachel nosed up into the driveway.

"How'd it go, Lady Luck?" asked Zachary with a teasing grin.

"I'm afraid my luck's just taken a turn for the worse," replied Bree miserably.

"Why? What happened? Was it us? Did we mess it up?" Rachel gazed at her apologetically.

Zachary was watching his friend. "You told him the truth," he said.

Bree nodded. "Well, you know what they say: A fool and her heart are soon parted."

Zachary and Rachel exchanged bewildered glances. "What are you talking about, Bree?"

Bree slumped against the wall and stared at them glumly. "Tonight, I fell in love."

What Bree should have said, was:"Tonight, I *realized* I've fallen in love." Notwithstanding, this correction wouldn't have made any difference; by the time Zachary finally drove Bree home, he was as much bewildered as he was before he'd attempted to pry the evening's details from her.

Bree closed her eyes and rested her head against the seat as the car turned down Alexandra Street.

"Hey! Isn't that Richard Bell?"

Bree's eyes snapped open and her heart gave a hard lurch behind her rib cage. She pressed her face against the glass of the passenger door window.

She spied him immediately—spied *them*. The blond woman with the tanned face and healthy, white-toothed smile was all too recognizable. The two of them were laughing, Richard with a pizza box tucked under his arm

The Camera-Shy Cupid

and Sandy Masterson leaning against his motorcycle, twirling the helmet in her hands. Bree glanced up at the flashing sign above them: PEEZA!

"Do you want to stop and say hello?"

"No," said Bree quickly. "Just keep driving." She slithered down in her seat and covered the side of her face with her hand.

Zachary's brows shot up. "Are you . . . hiding?"

"No, I just have a, uh, headache," lied Bree. She touched her stomach gently. "I-I don't feel so good."

In truth, this wasn't much of a lie; for suddenly she really did begin to feel ill. Nonetheless, despite her nausea and dizziness, Bree did manage to scowl at the passing couple. She glanced over just in time to see Richard slide the pizza into his saddlebag. Sandy Masterson straddled the motorcycle seat behind him and wrapped her arms possessively about his waist.

Oh, Bree, you're a fool, all right. She groaned to herself and looked away.

Chapter Twelve

Bree lay across the couch, unshowered, still in her "Sting Like a Bee" pajamas (a prize she'd won at one of the staff parties). She reached up her arms and yawned drowsily, too lethargic even to finish the stretch. Her laziness was compounded by the singular activity in which she'd been engaged for the past two hours. With the television remote control firmly in her grip, she pressed her thumb down on the channel-changer button.

Talk shows, soap operas, music videos, commercials for laundry detergent and deodorant whizzed by. She thought back to the ravings of George Kane, that day in the reading department. *Oh, yes, television: this is what's keeping me alive, all right.* She paused at the twenty-four-hour weather channel.

"It's sunny skies in Boise, folks! And yes, you can expect this weather to last right up until this weekend!" spouted the cheery-faced man with the pompadour toupee.

"Well, it's gloomy and foggy in here," grumbled Bree,

switching the channel. The remote dropped out of her hand and she raised her head slightly, her eyes focusing on the screen.

The theme music from "The Camera-Shy Cupid" quickly drifted in, and as quickly, faded. The camera zoomed in on Grey Blaine and Stan Adams. Patti Cameron strolled in and the restaurant set came into view. Bree sat up, her gaze immediately zeroing in on a central table where a man conversed with his slim dinner partner, a woman with jet black hair and very dark eye makeup. The woman smiled; the man laughed, seeming happy and quite at ease. Bree's heart performed a small flip-flop as the man whose face she now recognized turned slightly toward the camera.

Richard.

Bree watched with fascination as Lori glided onto the scene. Her expression was deadpan still, panic visible in the shifting of her eyes and the stiff unnaturalness of her movements. Bree guessed this was maybe her first day on the job; the station was playing last season's "The Camera-Shy Cupid" reruns. She watched Richard, reading his lips. Bree laughed aloud as she interpreted the word: "cantaloupe."

The phone rang. Bree reluctantly stood up and traipsed into the kitchen to answer it.

"Hi. It's Zachary."

"Hi."

"You sitting down?"

Bree pulled out the stool and sat down. She didn't like the tone in his voice, or the way the hair at the top of her scalp suddenly prickled to attention. "What's up, Zachary?"

"Well, I don't know if this is good news or bad news," began Zachary hesitantly. "I just got a call from Penny Dowling."

Bree grimaced. What now?

"You're out of the Honey-Chew commercial."

"What?"

"Look, I don't know what happened the other night—"

"Wait a second—"

"Apparently, they're going with someone else. I looked over the contract, and I think we might be able to fight it. But the 'Camera-Shy Cupid' contract, as you already know, is a one-way option."

" 'The Camera-Shy Cupid'? You mean they're *firing* me?" Bree stared at the phone, incredulous.

There was a long pause on the other end. "Bree, what exactly happened between you and Philippe Descartes?"

The doorbell buzzed.

"Hold on a second. Someone's at the door." Bree set the phone down, and dazedly tramped across the room. Unthinking, she unlatched the door and swung it open.

"Hello."

Bree blinked, startled. "What are you doing here?"

Richard's dour expression immediately changed into an amused grin as he took in her "Sting Like a Bee" pajamas and disheveled appearance.

"Gee, I should have brought along my 'Camera-Shy Cupid' slippers. The two of us could've solved mysteries while shooting photographs of women with Sideshow Bob hair."

Bree's hand went to her mussed locks, unsuccessfully attempting to tame the flyaway curls. She flushed beneath his wolfish gaze, a look she'd come to recognize—and grown to dislike—these past couple of weeks.

"I came to find out why you suddenly decided to bow out of the Honey-Chew commercial." His grin suddenly disappeared. He regarded her levelly.

"But I didn't—"

The Camera-Shy Cupid 159

Richard slipped inside.

"Well, why don't you just come in," Bree growled under her breath.

Richard glanced over at the TV, and raised his eyebrows. "Getting some pointers for next season?"

"I don't think I'll be needing any pointers for next season," said Bree. "If you don't mind, I'm on the phone—"

"No, go right ahead. I don't mind." Richard sat down on the couch and put his feet up on the coffee table.

"Just make yourself at home," she muttered between clenched teeth.

Richard looked up with a grin. "Do I get a pair of pajamas, too?"

Bree glanced down at herself, suddenly aware of her casual attire. Her bare feet stared up at her, and she fought down a blush of self-consciousness. What was she embarrassed about? This was her own apartment; she could do whatever she pleased. Her gaze shifted over to Richard, who was now engrossed in the "Camera-Shy Cupid" rerun on TV. She rolled her eyes and strode briskly into the bedroom. She grabbed her housecoat and shrugged it on, catching her reflection in the closet mirror.

Oh, just great! Do you think you could look any worse? She rubbed the sleep out of her eyes, and ran her fingers through her shaggy Raggedy Ann curls, but to no avail. Just a quick jump in the shower—she remembered then that she had left Zachary still hanging on the other end of the phone. She sighed. Her timing had never been great. Here was this attractive, charming man sitting in the next room, a man who seemed somehow capable of jangling every nerve in her body. What must he think of her? What time was it? Afternoon, she supposed. And here she was still in her pajamas—

Bree's stomach suddenly tightened, and her pulse began

to race angrily. *What's wrong with you? Why are you letting this guy get to you like this? What do you care what he thinks of you?* Bree demanded silently. She took a last glimpse of herself in the mirror, pursed her lips, and walked determinedly out of the bedroom.

She shot a brief look in Richard's direction, but saw that he was still absorbed by the "Camera-Shy Cupid" episode on television.

"Hi, Zachary. Sorry about that," she said into the phone. Her voice was barely audible.

"You okay? You sound funny all of a sudden."

Bree swiveled around so that her back was to Richard. "No, I'm fine," she said a little louder.

"Anyway, this firing business—maybe it has to do with you turning down that role on 'The Camera-Shy Cupid.' I don't know. But Tom Bronfmann called me up last night and said they won't be needing you anymore. He went on about budget cuts or something, but I have a feeling that was just an excuse."

"Oh, well," said Bree resignedly.

"Geez, you're taking this pretty well."

"I still have my old job, right?"

"Yes, of course. But you know, there's something fishy going on here. I can just feel it," said Zachary. "I wish you'd tell me what went on between you and Philippe Descartes. He's a very influential guy, you know. But he's not worth breaking your heart over. He's a fool if he can't see what a great girl you are."

I'm the fool, groaned Bree silently. "Oh, don't worry about me, Zachary. I'll-I'll manage."

"Hey, you don't sound so good. Why don't you come over here and I'll take you out to lunch— Oh, it's after two. How about I come over there after work, and you and Rachel and I go out to dinner?"

The Camera-Shy Cupid   161

"I don't know—" She glanced over at Richard. "I think I'm just going to brood here for a while."

"You sure? Look, I can get off early, in say, an hour and a half? I'll come over and cheer you up. I bet you're not even dressed yet."

Bree grimaced. "As a matter of fact—"

"I'll see you in a bit, then." And he hung up.

Bree slid off the stool and placed the receiver back in the cradle.

"So? Tell me what changed your mind."

"Huh?" Bree looked over at Richard.

Richard turned off the television. "Why aren't you doing the Honey-Chew commercial?"

"I'm going to take a shower." She took a step toward the bathroom.

Richard stood up and lunged at her, his hand clamping down on her arm. "It's not because of me, is it? Because you know, sometimes I say things—"

"Of course not," said Bree, shrugging off his grip. And staring up into his boyishly handsome face, she suddenly realized that even with all her protests, she'd had real fun these past two weeks. And it dawned on her that she was truthfully disappointed that it was all ending.

"They changed their minds," she told him. "I guess I wasn't the right girl for the job, after all."

"Of course you're the right girl. You know, for a moment I thought—" His voice trailed off into a deep furrowing frown. He looked confused.

"You thought what?"

"I don't understand. You and I—we're perfect for each other."

Bree stared at him. "Excuse me?"

And much to her astonishment she saw the color suddenly rise to his cheeks. He shifted his gaze to his feet and scratched his head.

"I mean, we work so well together," he mumbled.

"We *worked* so well together," she amended. "I'm going back to my old job, as of Monday," she said. Her cheeriness sounded artificial and forced to her own ears.

Richard's brows drew together, and for a moment Bree thought he was angry. But he nodded, his lips spreading into a grim smile. "I'm happy for you," he said without conviction. He rubbed his hands together. "Yes, we should celebrate. Go have your shower and I'll take you to the art museum."

"The museum?"

"They're showing a photography exhibit this week. Chariss Lemby. You know, she does all those blurry close-ups?"

Hadn't Philippe mentioned some photography exhibit? "Yes, I've heard of her. But—"

"Hurry up. If we get there before three-thirty it's free."

"And heaven knows I can't afford it, now. Not on my budget." Bree sighed.

"What—you think sitcom extras are millionaires? And the season's almost over. . . ." He paused, looking slightly wistful.

"Well, at least you can look forward to the Honey-Chew commercials," Bree pointed out. She mustered her best cheerful smile. "And there's always a chance you might land another role on 'Sting Like a Bee.' You never know."

"Hmmm . . . fat chance." He chewed on his lip, stroking his chin thoughtfully. "At least I managed to sell my—" He cut himself off abruptly, his eyes suddenly taking on a guarded look. He shifted his gaze about her apartment, chewing on his lip as if to ruminate on some stray thought.

But Bree could feel an element of secrecy suddenly mushroom in the air between them, and she regarded

The Camera-Shy Cupid

Richard curiously. She watched him pull out, on impulse, one of her books from the bookshelf. He flipped through the pages, not really reading, it seemed to Bree—but hiding.

Hiding from what? she wondered. Certainly, in these two weeks she'd known him, this man had exhibited those qualities she'd imagined all actors needed to possess to get ahead in this business: an overabundance of confidence and mulish single-mindedness, not to mention an ego the size of Texas. And yet, there was something almost shy about him now as he stood reading in her living room. No, not shy, but . . . reserved, contemplative. Beneath that boyish, joking cloak he insisted on wearing, she suspected there lay a man of genuine candor and sincerity, a man who was highly sensitive and intelligent.

"You wouldn't happen to suscribe to the *Boise Wrestling Mania Guide,* would you?" he said staring at her latest copy of *The Heart of Art Magazine.* "Machete Mike is supposed to be fighting the Forensic Scientist this afternoon. Predicted to be quite a bloodbath." He grinned.

Bree smirked, her last thoughts about this man suddenly vanishing in a puff of smoke. *Sensitive? Intelligent? Pah!* She sighed and shook her head. "I'm going to take a shower."

They were inside the museum studying a large, poster-size black-and-white photograph of a man dressed in a suit and tie and sunglasses, walking toward the camera. The subject's fuzzy outline contrasted with the sharply defined background, which depicted an outdoor café scene. A young man and woman, sporting partially shaved heads and earrings and leather jackets, held hands across the table, their faces very close. To Bree, the photo gave off the sensation of eavesdropping, for she suddenly felt very much like a voyeur peeping into someone's window.

"I almost feel like I shouldn't be looking at this photograph—like I'm invading their privacy or something," said Richard.

Bree didn't say anything, though she wondered idly whether she was telegraphing her thoughts, or if Richard was able to read minds. She thought it strange that with every photograph they'd scrutinized thus far, Richard's comments had mostly mirrored her own. Was he trying to impress her? she wondered. He *was* being awfully considerate, and she found she was truly enjoying his company. She snuck a quick sidelong glance at him. But he was already immersed in the adjacent photo, his features contorted into an expression of thoughtful concentration.

Bree moved beside him.

Why, it was the BBA Production building! Bree read the inscripted title beneath the frame: A HARD DAY'S WORK. She peered at it closer, and was instantly taken aback by who she saw in the background. Could it possibly be—?

"Good afternoon, Mademoiselle Gaston, Monsieur Bell," interrupted an accented voice behind them.

They turned to face Philippes Descartes. He wore a charcoal gray gabardine suit that hung miraculously well on his slender frame. His chiseled European face was unsmiling, but his expression was not impolite.

"Hello, Philippe," said Bree, flushing. She felt suddenly very miserable standing there.

"Checking out the local museum, Mr. Descartes?" said Richard, extending his hand. Philippe shook it, staring at Richard with such an intensity that Bree thought maybe he was trying to hypnotize Richard. Richard, on the other hand, met the Frenchman's gaze without so much as a blink.

Philippe turned to Bree, smiling faintly. "I understand now." He gestured to the woman he was with, a tall,

The Camera-Shy Cupid

leggy brunet wearing very dark sunglasses. The woman pointed to the exit.

Richard squinted at the woman. "Is that—?"

Philippe shrugged. "I'm afraid I must be going." His tone was cold and insincere. "It was a pleasure running into you both." And he walked over to catch up to his date, who was already pushing open the glass exit doors.

"That was Paula!" exclaimed Richard.

"Paula? You mean . . . your old extra partner?"

"Yeah, Paula Fizzner. Boy, does she look great!" His blue eyes twinkled and he smiled. "Second-best acting partner I ever had."

"Second best?"

Richard cocked a derisive eyebrow at her, as if he couldn't believe she'd ask such a question. "Well, you're the best, of course."

"I *was* the best," Bree corrected, angry at herself for flushing at his compliment. "Thank you, but I wouldn't say I was—"

"Hey, did you look at this photograph? Anyone look familiar?" Richard grinned.

Bree turned back to the photograph titled "A Hard Day's Work," and immediately zoomed in on what had startled her before Philippe had interrupted them. Yes, there was no mistake about it. There she was in the background, strolling alongside Zachary, her head tilted back, laughing, perhaps at some silly joke her friend had just told her. From the brilliant orangey-yellow-red coloring of the leaves on the maples and oaks, she guessed the photograph had been taken sometime last fall. *What a coincidence,* she thought, shifting her gaze to the slightly blurred foreground. The familiar park fountain cherub spouted water in the background, while a young man sat on a bench reading and eating a sandwich. Bree's eyes suddenly widened as she brought her face closer to inspect the photo. She looked over at Richard, then back at the photo. Could it be? Her throat made an involuntary gurglelike gasp.

"That's you," she said in astonishment.

Richard pointed to the background, smiling. "And that is you. Some coincidence, huh?"

Bree didn't know what to say. A man strolled over to stand next to them. He frowned at the photograph, glanced at Bree, then returned to the photo. Bree ducked her head as if to hide, and Richard looked over at her, the corner of his lips curving up in amusement.

As she started to move over to the next photograph on display, she suddenly remembered Zachary. "Oh!" She slapped her forehead. "I forgot Zachary was coming to see me." She glanced at her watch. "If I run over to his office now, I might still catch—"

"Well, well! I thought I'd find you here!" a voice pitched between them.

Bree spun around and found herself face to face with a dazzling set of teeth. Sandy Masterson stood before them, her hands on her hips, her tanned face beaming more than usual. Her gaze shifted to Bree, and her smile broadened. Bree observed that her eyes, a brilliant hazel green this time, matched perfectly the color of her dress—what there was of it, anyway.

"Richie and I were just saying yesterday what a coincidence it was—both of you being in that photograph." Sandy turned musingly to the photo on the wall. "You didn't even know each other then, did you?"

"No." The corners of Bree's lips tightened. So he'd already seen the exhibit; he knew this photograph was here, and he just wanted to see her reaction.

"Oh, Richie! I have the best news!" Sandy Masterson leaped into his arms. "You're not going to believe it!"

Bree turned to them, her tone icy. "Yes, well, I have to be going."

Richard looked at her, his face very still. He seemed about to say something, his lips twitching uncertainly for a moment. But Sandy squeezed his arm, leaning against him happily, and Richard winced, looking suddenly sheepish.

"Lucky for me I found you," said Sandy brightly.

"Yes, lucky," Bree murmured under her breath. She smiled at Sandy coldly. "Unfortunately, I can't stay. I have to go meet someone." And before she'd even finished uttering these words, Bree was already striding swiftly across the room toward the museum exit.

Once outside, her iciness melted, quickly gushing into anger. She was suddenly conscious of the pounding of her own heart, her lungs aching as she ran down the street, past the zoo, making her way toward the BBA Production building. *How dare he?* she spat in silent frustration. But she immediately frowned at this thought.

How dare he *what*, exactly? Lie to her? No, that wasn't what was bothering her. He had led her on, deceived her into believing he cared for her. But, wait—had he really misled her? Or was it she who had misled herself?

Bree paused for a brief moment to glance over at the cherub spewing water into the park fountain, and visualized Richard sitting there, reading and eating his lunch.

Two weeks ago they hadn't even met. But to Bree, it felt as though a lifetime had passed since they'd first sat together on the restaurant set of "The Camera-Shy Cupid." And it seemed now as if Richard had always been there, lurking just out of focus in the foreground, like a street sign she'd missed because she'd been driving too fast.

And all of a sudden the truth dawned on her. That first

day on the set of "The Camera-Shy Cupid"—yes, that was when she'd begun to fall in love with Richard Bell.

Only now, it was too late; she'd been fired from "The Camera-Shy Cupid," and she would no longer be working on the Honey-Chew commercial, and, she realized, she probably wouldn't ever see Richard again.

Oh, what a blind fool you are, Bree Gaston, she thought miserably.

"Hey! I was just about to pack up and head over to your place," said Zachary, looking up from his desk. He gazed at Bree, frowning. "What'd you do? Run all the way here? You're all flushed."

"It's hot outside."

"I'm going to be a minute—whoa, while you're here ... you might want to take a look at this." He fished a file folder from his desk drawer and handed it to her.

"What's this?" She opened it, eyeing the contract.

"Our writer friend Rudolph Gotham finally sent us back the contracts. All signed—but read the added provisional statement at the bottom." And before Bree could read it, he went on. "I guess this guy's really serious about protecting his privacy. He refuses to meet with the story production heads, and he doesn't even want a byline."

"Really? That's a bit odd—"

"Oh, but here's the best part. He says he'll only deal, get this ... through *me*."

Bree eyed her friend doubtfully. "Zachary, quit fooling around."

Zachary shook his head, his soft brown eyes wide and sincere. "No, I'm telling you the truth." He gazed at the contract thoughtfully. "Strange thing that he would pick me, of all people. I'm just a go-between, after all. I have

The Camera-Shy Cupid 169

no real authority. So how'd he get my name? It doesn't appear anywhere here in the contract."

"So, what does Cantrell say? He must be fuming."

Zachary chuckled. "You know how he is with writers. He can't stand to relinquish any control to them. But BBA really wants Rudolph Gotham—whoever he is—and, well, Earl Cantrell is vying for an Emmy next year."

"Isn't he every year?" Bree grinned. "Do I hear a promotion buzzing your way?"

Zachary snorted. "Yeah, when the moon crashes into the sun, and aliens take over television."

"They already have," said Bree with a laugh.

Zachary chuckled, then cupped his chin, a faraway gaze coming into his eyes. "I've been seriously thinking about making some career changes, Bree. Word got out that I was representing your friend, Richard Bell, and some ideas about conflict of interest started to crop up...." He grimaced.

"You're not thinking of leaving BBA, are you?" said Bree in astonishment.

"Bree, you know I've always wanted to get back into the agenting business. And with Rudolph Gotham as a client—"

"He wants you to represent him?"

"That's what it looks like. And get this. Yesterday, I got a call from a woman named Sandy Masterson—"

"Yes, I know her. She's an extra on 'The Camera-Shy Cupid' and 'Sting Like a Bee.' " Bree tried to mask the contempt in her voice. Contempt? Or was it just jealousy?

But Zachary's enthusiasm had already taken flight, and he did not notice Bree's sudden change in tone. "Well, apparently she landed the lead role in the Honey-Chew commercials, and she wants to employ me as her agent." Zachary shook his head. "The guy who used to represent her fled the country on some drug-related charge— Aw, Bree. I'm sorry. I wasn't thinking—"

Bree winced a smile, and dismissed his apology with a wave of her hand. "No, it's all right, Zachary. Really. That job didn't mean anything to me. I'm just surprised they chose Sandy Masterson, that's all," she said, realizing her jealousy was showing all too plainly.

"Oh? You don't think she's that good an actress?"

"She's—she's not right for Richard," she blurted out.

Zachary gazed at her quizzically. But then, his puzzlement gave way to a sudden understanding grin. There was a teasing laughter in the curved lips. "Oh, I'm starting to see now."

"See what?" she retorted defensively. "No, it's not what you think—"

"And here I thought you'd fallen for this Philippe Descartes, while all this time you—"

"Don't say it." Bree pointed a warning finger at him.

"But, Bree, if you're in love with Rich—"

"Don't say it."

"But you're in love with him—"

"I'm not listening!" Bree put her hands over her ears.

"You're in love with Richard Bell!" said Zachary, raising his voice almost to a shout.

Bree stood up and strolled about the room, humming loudly.

"Admit it! For once in your life, be honest with yourself!"

Bree started singing "The Star-Spangled Banner," her voice lifting to an off-key shriek.

"Say it! Say you're in love with Richard Bell—"

"What the devil is going on here?" A balding man with a thin mustache stood gazing at them from the doorway. Bree turned around slowly, halting in mid-chorus.

The Camera-Shy Cupid

"Hey, Chalmers! We can hear you all the way down the hall."

Bree bit her lip, watching her friend's face turn an embarrassed rosy hue. She stifled a giggle and shot Zachary an apologetic grimace.

"Er, sorry, Earl. We were just, er, rehearsing."

"Rehearsing for what? 'Who's Afraid of the Star-Spangled Banner'?" He guffawed at his own pathetic wit, then immediately crumpled his features into a stern reprimand. "This is not an acting studio, Chalmers."

"No, of course not. I'm sorry for the noise, Earl," Zachary apologized.

"Yes, well—" Earl Cantrell tucked his tie into his waistband. "Keep it down from now on, all right?" And he marched away with an important look on his pale, flabby face.

Zachary looked at Bree, and they burst out laughing.

"That guy doesn't like you very much," said Bree.

"There's another reason why I should leave."

Bree sighed. "I'll miss you."

"You'll get over it." Zachary reached for his briefcase, and stood up. "Let's get out of here. So what do you feel like? Chinese? Indian? Pizza? We have to stop and get some takeout. All we've got at home is bread." He sighed. "You know, I could call up Richard, and you and Rachel and I could double-date—"

"Don't you dare!"

"Aha! You *are* in love with him. Admit it."

"I'm not admitting anything. It isn't true."

"So how come you're turning all red?"

Bree let out an exasperated breath, and glowered at him.

"Is it that you're afraid he doesn't feel the same way about you? Is that it? That can easily be straightened out." Zachary sighed. "Why do you always have to complicate things, Bree? Look, I can give you his number—or better yet, I'll give him *your* number."

He already has my number, she thought. "Zachary, leave it alone, will you?" He's in love with someone else. "Promise me you'll leave it alone."

"But why not just call—?"

"Promise me." She gazed at him earnestly.

"Okay, okay. I promise." He shook his head, not understanding.

As they stepped onto the elevator, Zachary leaned over and whispered in her ear: "Why can't you just admit you're in love with him?"

The man standing next to Bree, having overheard this, shifted nervously. He ran his finger inside the collar of his shirt. Bree gave him an embarrassed grin, and he returned it with a warm glowing smile. As the elevator doors opened he turned to her.

"Hi, I'm Mark Jenkins from the story editing department. Would you like—?"

"Sorry, her heart's already taken," said Zachary, steering her away. "Only she won't admit it."

Oh, I admit it, sighed Bree silently, *fool that I am.*

Chapter Thirteen

Bree set the popcorn between her legs and switched on the television. She flicked to Channel 4 and waited. Her heartbeat quickened, and she realized her palms were sweating. The phone rang. She looked over at it in irritation. It persisted, and after the sixth ring, she set the bowl of popcorn down on the coffee table and plodded into the kitchen.

"Bree? You watching?"

"Yes, Zachary. I just turned it on," said Bree patiently. All week, Zachary had been reminding her that the new spring season's "The Camera-Shy Cupid" was airing this Friday. Apparently, the first three weeks' episodes included the restaurant scenes. She had to admit that the prospect of seeing herself on television gave her a tiny thrill.

She recalled that when she'd run into Lori that day she'd returned the dress to Mrs. H. some months ago.

"I can't believe they canceled your contract. They got

rid of Sandy's partner, too. I don't know what they're thinking, putting those two together. It's you and Richie who belong together."

Bree shrugged nonchalantly, and gave Lori her best upbeat smile. "This business is not for me, anyway." She told Lori about her job in the reading department, and the young woman looked a little less upset. They chatted until the man in the ripped jeans called everyone onto the set.

Mrs. H. wrapped her big arms around her and gave her some motherly advice. "Sometimes you young people baffle me. You have to look past your own nose to see what's going on in the rest of your face."

"... been almost seven months." Zachary's voice sliced through her thoughts and brought her careening back into the present. "He's still single, you know."

She knew who he meant. "Hmmm... just barely. I heard he's now engaged to Sandy Masterson." Bree couldn't bring herself to conceal the misery in her voice. Richard had her number; he knew where she lived. If he'd wanted to talk to her he certainly had the opportunity.

"Since when do you read the tabloids? You know that stuff's just rumor. Oh! I think it's starting. Rachel's taping it for you. Talk to you later. 'Bye!"

The episode was a silly one, with Astrid Kettleby, a runway fashion model, appearing as a guest star. Grey Blaine had been hired to photograph her, and he and his assistant, played by Stan Adams, spent the entire episode arguing over a controversial tattoo they'd observed in a very odd place on her body. Now their friend, played by Olivia Williams, confessed to also having a tattoo in the same place. Naturally, Grey Blaine and Stan Adams's curiosity get the better of them and they suddenly become very interested in their woman friend.

They'd butchered the original script idea that Bree remembered recommending, and for her, the dialogue

The Camera-Shy Cupid 175

sounded flat and uninteresting. But the presence of the veteran actress, Patti Cameron, made up for the episode's lack of charm.

Bree waited, her stomach fluttering with butterflies, for the scene to switch to the restaurant set. But the show faded out and quickly segued into a commercial. Bree sighed and shoveled a handful of popcorn into her mouth. She paused in mid-chew, staring at the screen.

There was Sandy Masterson strolling down a quaint cobbled street. They had dressed her in a plain cotton sundress, and had toned down the brassy blondness of her hair, transforming her into a nice, natural, country woman. But her walk exuded allure, the plain sundress still managing to accentuate her ample curves. She stopped to browse the window of a local grocery store. A shot of a candy bar, the name Honey-Chew filling the screen. The camera caught Sandy's reaction. An overreaction, thought Bree smugly, tasting a twinge of bitterness on her tongue as she watched the rest of the commercial unfold. The store owner was reminiscent of a Mr. McGoo/Archie Bunker type. (Later, Bree would find out that the actor playing the store owner was none other than Virgil Halwig, Zachary's ex-client from New York.) Bree liked him. She listened and watched as Sandy asked about the Honey-Chew candy bar in the window. Then Richard entered the store. Bree drew in a sharp breath.

When he looked directly into the camera, Bree's heart skipped a beat, and a rush of heat suddenly surged through her. He spoke a line to Sandy, his blue eyes steady and fearless and full of humor. The camera loved him, and Bree knew that he and his boyish charm had snagged not only her, but every female member of the television audience watching.

The commercial ended there, the first of the six Honey-Chew episodes. Bree continued to stare at the television screen, the thoughts in her head blurring her vision as the commercials flashed by. She knew where the commercial would ultimately lead, and she was thinking that she couldn't bear to see Richard and Sandy Masterson kiss. Bree brushed her own lips with her fingertips. Why couldn't she forget him? She emitted a loud, frustrated groan. *Get over it! You blew your chance. He's with Sandy Masterson now.*

"The Camera-Shy Cupid" returned, but Bree's glumness dulled her excitement. She watched as the camera shifted points of view, then pulled back and panned the restaurant. She grimaced as she recognized herself, garbed in that ridiculous green Spandex dress. Instinctively, she drew her sweater tightly over her shirt. No wonder Richard was staring at her that way.

They had edited it well, thought Bree, impressed, recalling the retakes they'd had to shoot that day because of her ineptness. *But didn't I warn them I wasn't an actor?*

Yet Lori and Zachary had been right about one thing: Bree sensed it even through the screen; it was like a field of electricity generated between herself and Richard, a "spark," as Lori had put it. But maybe she was just imagining it—wishing it was there? Richard was, after all, an actor; this is what he did for a living, and this is what he was doing: acting.

Bree watched, reading their silent words, catching snatches of their conversation with the occasional interspersed "cantaloupe," "watermelon," "I love—"? Her jaw dropped. What had Richard said to her? Now she'd said it. Why, it appeared as though she had just told him that she loved him! "I love you"; yes, those were the words that her lips had formed. But she'd never—

Bree searched in her memory for those extra keywords: "cantaloupe," "watermelon," *"elephant shoes"* ... She

The Camera-Shy Cupid 177

mouthed the two latter words again. *Oh, no! He tricked me!* The scene ended, and Bree jumped up and rushed over to the mirror in the front hall.

"Elephant shoes," she repeated aloud to her reflection, watching her lips closely. She squeezed her eyes shut and slapped her forehead. To a lip reader, the words looked deceptively like "I love you."

How many times had she uttered those words? She moaned as she recalled the other restaurant scenes. She'd certainly said it often enough. Anger suddenly rose in her chest. That creep! He knew exactly what she was saying all along. He'd been stringing her along, making her look like a fool.

But he'd said it, too, hadn't he? He'd said it that night of their date—after he'd dropped her off. They'd both said it.

It didn't mean anything, you twit. Bree frowned at her reflection. It meant exactly what it sounded like: "Elephant shoes"—footwear for very large mammals. Nothing more. She sighed dismally and returned to the couch. But the "Camera-Shy Cupid" theme song was playing and the credits flashed on the screen. Bree glimpsed her name; it appeared alongside Richard's in white type.

The phone rang. Bree lunged for it.

It was her folks, calling all the way from Ontario, Canada.

"Who was that young man, dear? You didn't tell me you were seeing anyone! Just a minute... your father wants to know if this young man has a regular job. Oh, Eldridge! Your father really didn't care for that outfit you were wearing. It might have been a little, you know, snug. You're really not wearing those kinds of dresses these days, are you?"

"That wasn't my dress. Mom. The studio—"

"Oh, darling, I'm so proud of you! My baby, on television! Now tell me, what's this young man's name? He's so handsome, too! And I could tell right away that he adores you. Maybe you could invite him up here. It's been so long since we've seen you, Bree. I'd almost given up on you marrying...."

Bree patiently let her mother ramble on, knowing full well that by the time she hung up, she wouldn't be able to get a word in edgewise. She'd write later and tell her that there was nothing between her and Richard. She could already see the disappointment in her mother's face. Maybe by the time she got around to sending the letter she'd be seriously dating someone....

Bree snorted. For the past seven months she'd dated all of five men, and they were five nice, attractive men. They'd all liked her, too, wanting to see her again—even after she'd accidentally dumped a mug of steaming coffee in one date's lap (he suffered only minor burns, thankfully). She'd gone out for a romantic candlelight dinner with one of the readers in her department and had somehow managed to set fire to the man's tie. And then there was the man from the story editing department. After riding the new Super Duper Scooper Rollercoaster at Boise Park, she'd embarrassed herself by vomiting all over his new suede jacket.

And yet, despite these clumsy incidents they'd all wanted to see her again. It baffled Bree, but still more baffling was her reluctance to accept their invitations. Oh, she knew what the reason was, but she did not like to admit it to herself. And, of course, this only infuriated and frustrated her all the more.

Let him go, she told herself. *Richard's with Sandy Masterson now. He's living his life, so why don't you just forget about him and live yours?*

Bree sighed aloud and went to turn off the TV just as the phone rang again. She let it ring and shambled off to the bathroom to run a nice hot bubble bath where she could drown out her thoughts.

Bree sagged in her chair. It wasn't a very good day. The scripts she'd read were awful; one particular manuscript was actually handwritten in an illegible scrawl, with curlicues on the capital letters, and little circles above the i's. Another, frustratingly enough, was missing about four pages in the middle—and the very last page. She consulted her watch. It told her that she had less than fifteen minutes left to her shift. She closed her eyes and kneaded the dull ache in her temples.

"Bree Gaston?"

Bree opened her eyes tiredly and looked up at the courier. "Yes?"

"Package for you. Sign here, please."

She wrote her signature and the young courier handed her a manila envelope. Too weary to show any surprise (never before had she received a manuscript personally addressed to her), she turned it over in her hands for a few moments. Distractedly she noted the absence of any return address. *I'll look at it tomorrow,* she thought, glancing at her watch. But the strength of her curiosity overwhelmed her, and she found herself tearing open the envelope.

The name immediately jumped out at her, and she sat up in her chair with a jolt. Rudolph Gotham. What was this man doing, sending her his manuscript? She began to read, this time with new eagerness and anticipation.

But as she flipped to the second page, Bree realized the teleplay was not written for "Sting Like a Bee" or "The Camera-Shy Cupid" or any of the other, more minor BBA shows. The characters were original, the first scene taking place in a pizza parlor where the main male character worked. And there was something vaguely familiar about the characters, their dialogue sounded almost too true to life. Bree continued to read, her attention riveted to the story that unfolded, fascinated and intrigued by the romance slowly developing between the two main characters.

She was interrupted by her coworkers in the surrounding cubicles who were preparing to leave for the day. Bree closed the script and slipped it back into the envelope. She gazed at it, thought for a moment, and hastily stuffed it into her book bag. It was addressed to her, after all, wasn't it? She'd give it to Zachary after she finished reading the script, she reasoned. Zachary was Rudolph Gotham's agent—and yet, for some reason, the author had chosen to send it to her. But why her? And more important, how did he know her? How did he know Bree worked in the reading department? Who was this mysterious Rudolph Gotham?

Bree was still puzzling over this as she walked across the parking lot to her old green Rabbit. She climbed in, threw her book bag onto the passenger seat and keyed the ignition. The car whined and sputtered. She tried again, pumping the gas lightly. Her old Rabbit jerked into a simpering roar, then petered out into obstinate silence.

"Come on, girl," she coaxed.

The car ululated a harsh complaint, whimpered, then abruptly lapsed into a quiet death. Bree slumped over the steering wheel with a groan. It wasn't as if the mechanic at the shop hadn't warned her this might happen."

"You sure you want me to try an' fix 'er up? She looks like she needs a permanent rest," the mechanic had said, gazing at the Rabbit uncertainly. "It'd be like putting a Band-Aid on a slit throat. Sorry to say, but this baby's about decapitated, miss."

But Bree insisted. It had taken almost all of her paycheck from the extra work she'd done on "The Camera-

The Camera-Shy Cupid

Shy Cupid'' and "Sting Like a Bee," but to her, it was worth it.

However, now that she was stranded here in the parking lot, she wasn't so sure. Why hadn't she taken Zachary's advice and invested in a new car, like every normal, sensible human being?

The manila envelope, half hanging out of her book bag, caught her eye. Bree reached over and retrieved it. She turned it over in her hands wonderingly, then pulled out the manuscript. Before she knew it, she was flipping to the page of the story where she'd left off, and began to reimmerse herself in the script.

Bree read to the end of it, gripping the script in her hand. She didn't know whether to laugh or cry; for it was, despite its maudlin sentimentality, a strangely beautiful script. She turned to the last page and read it, aloud this time:

" ' . . . when I'm around you I find myself hiding who I really am, how I feel inside. Who is this person? I ask myself. Because this guy talking to you—I don't know him. What makes him—' "

" '—say the things he says?' " A voice suddenly cut in, and Bree jumped, startled. " 'Do the things he does when he's around you? Why must he act the fool when you're near?' "

Bree sat up slowly, staring at the script in her hand. The voice outside her window went on quickly:

" 'Like a lens in a camera, everything seems to blur out of focus when I'm around you, and I'm always fumbling for the right words to tell you how I feel. But always the wrong ones come out.'

" 'Well, I'm telling you now that everything has started to come into focus, and I'm no longer afraid to let you see who Kenneth Murray really is—how he truly feels about you.' "

Bree looked over and stared at Richard. "How—? What—?" Her mouth worked but her words stuck in her throat. The script trembled a little in her hands.

"Hi. Let me introduce myself." Richard extended his hand through the open window. Bree, too stunned to think, clasped it meekly. "I'm Richard Bell, also known as Rudolph Gotham."

"You? But that—that can't—" Bree stammered in astonishment.

Richard grinned, his clear blue eyes shining. He opened her door and knelt down. For an instant his brows knit together in earnestness, and his grin melted into a sweet, adoring smile. Bree glimpsed a sudden nervous glint in his eyes.

"You—? You're Rudolph Gotham?" said Bree.

"Let me finish. I want to tell you that I loved you from the start—that from the first day I saw you walk in wearing that ridiculous green dress—"

"That wasn't my dress," Bree interrupted. "And that's not in the script—"

Richard ignored her and continued, his eyes locked on hers. "You stirred something in me, a feeling that left me ... well, terrified. You entered my thoughts and stayed there. And as hard as I tried I could not get you out of my mind. In the middle of the afternoon, I found myself wondering what is she doing? What is she thinking? Is she wearing those cute 'Sting Like a Bee' pajamas—"

Bree flipped through the pages of the script with quaking fingers. "That's not here in the—"

"No." Richard reached up and clasped her hand. "It's not. Bree, I'm trying to tell you how I feel." He ran his fingers through his hair. "I tried running away from it, tried rationalizing all these feelings inside me, telling myself that it all meant nothing if Bree Gaston didn't feel the same way—"

The Camera-Shy Cupid   183

"Oh, Richard." Bree squeezed his hand, her heart thumping wildly against her rib cage.

"And I realized it didn't matter—that I had to let you know that I—" He suddenly broke off, wincing, an agonized expression splaying across his handsome features.

"What about Sunday? The papers said you were engaged—"

"We're friends, that's all. There's never been anything between Sandy and me." He looked up at her. "You can't believe everything you read. Well, except for this..." His voice trailed off, and he ran his fingers through his hair, staring down at his feet. "This is hard, you know? For once in my life, I-I meant every word I wrote—what ... what I just said."

Bree stared at him, not knowing how to respond. Her head was spinning, the blood pounding in her ears. She needed time to think, to focus.

An uncomfortable silence erupted between them. After a moment, Richard went to release her hand, but Bree held onto it, suddenly clasping it in hers tightly. She took a deep breath and compressed her lips for courage.

"Elephant shoes," she murmured softly.

Richard gazed at her, his mouth slowly widening into a grin. "Elephant shoes," he echoed. He stood up and pulled her out of the car, holding her close. "I love you, Bree Gaston."

"Cantaloupe," whispered Bree.

Richard cocked an eyebrow and frowned.

"I love you, too, Richard Bell—Rudolph Gotham, or whoever you are," she said, kissing him. She stopped suddenly. "But wait, does Zachary know that you and Rudolph Gotham are one and the same?"

A mischievous twinkle appeared in his eyes. "No, not yet. But actually, my real—"

Bree entwined her arms around his neck and kissed

him, pressing herself to him. She could feel Richard's heart beating in time with her own, and a great happiness welled inside her. For the first time in a long time she felt complete.

"You were saying?" she murmured huskily, as Richard nuzzled her ear, his lips trailing down to the hollow of her throat.

"My name: it's not . . ." He kissed her forehead. ". . . really Richard Bell." He kissed the tip of her nose. "It's actually . . ." He kissed her lips. "Richard Belavagt."

"What!?"

Richard laughed throatily and held her tightly. "Don't worry, my sweet." He kissed her soundly on the lips. "In time, it'll all come into focus."